THE LEE SHORE

By the same author

Stella and the Fireships
Mutiny in the Caribbean
The Malta Frigate
Seven Gun Broadside
The Quarterdeck Ladder

The Lee Shore

SHOWELL STYLES

WILLIAM KIMBER · LONDON

First published in 1986 by
WILLIAM KIMBER & CO. LIMITED
100 Jermyn Street, London SW1Y 6EE

© Showell Styles, 1986

ISBN 0-7183-0607-4

Photoset in North Wales by
Derek Doyle & Associates Mold, Clwyd
and printed in Great Britain by
Biddles Limited, Guildford and King's Lynn

Contents

		Page
I	The Secret Agent	7
II	Houat Island	27
III	Captain Cockburn's Duty	45
IV	The Landing	66
V	The Road to Valençay	89
VI	Toujours de l'Audace	113
VII	The Hurried Journey	135
VIII	The Mill at Callac	160

I

The Secret Agent

1

'And please to remember, señores,' said the Foreign Secretary finally and incisively, 'that the utmost secrecy must be observed.'

'The udmost zegrezy,' echoed the Baron de Kolli solemnly.

He and his companion went towards the door, which a footman was holding open; beside the Baron's bulky figure Don Felicito Maura, the younger of the two Spanish envoys, looked like a boy. In the doorway the Baron turned and struck a heroic attitude with one hand raised aloft.

'This year of eighteen hundred and ten shall be *annus mirabilis*!' he pronounced. 'In all the prayers of Spain it shall be remembered, and viz it the name of Milord Vezzley – *se lo prometo*!'

He swung on his heel and went out with Don Felicito. The footman, following, closed the door and the three men left in the room resumed their seats at the big table. The oldest of the three, Lord Melcombe, opened his mouth to speak and then closed it again, dissuaded by the expression of cold abstraction on the Marquess Wellesley's beak-nosed face; he sat back frowning uneasily and folded plump hands across his vast expanse of flowered-satin waistcoat. He was at this conference by the King's express command, King George being just now in a period of comparative sanity, but he owed that honour solely to His Majesty's discovery that his Gentleman of the Bedchamber was the same age as himself, 72. The Secretary of the Admiralty was the first to speak.

'Let us hope,' he said drily, 'that all the prayers of Spain will reach the saints with your name correctly pronounced, my lord.'

Wellesley darted an irritable glance at him but said nothing. John Croker was Dublin-born like himself and he endured Croker's quips with a tolerance he would have afforded no other commoner.

'Would you say De Kolli can keep a secret?' Croker went on. 'I'd be doubting it myself.'

'If he cannot, he faces the guillotine,' Wellesley said with a shrug. 'That should keep his mouth shut. But the British part in this enterprise must be no secret in Spain.'

Croker nodded, his thin dark face intent. 'The Royalists will flock to the aid of your brother in the Peninsula when they hear of it.'

'Just so. Lord Wellington needs every man he can get against Bonaparte's generals. But –' Wellesley turned to face the King's representative – 'what thinks Lord Melcombe of our plans? They will, I trust, satisfy His Majesty?'

His pale features were hard and expressionless as marble and there was something snake-like in the glitter of his narrowed eyes. Lord Melcombe found himself confused.

'S-satisfy?' he stammered. 'Well, as to that – well, dammit, hard to say, hard to say, y' know. For my own part –'

'Well?' snapped the Foreign Secretary as he paused.

'For my own part, my lord,' Melcombe went on, gathering confidence as he talked, 'I'd say it looks a damned chancy business. His Majesty – I have it from his own lips – looks upon it as aid extended by himself to a royal brother in sore straits. For that – and by your leave, my lord – it seems to me there's a lack of organisation, I don't see –'

'Wait,' Wellesley's icy tone halted him at once, 'I hardly think, Lord Melcombe, that you can have grasped our plan. Let me recapitulate. The two gentlemen who have just left us, envoys of our ally Spain, have requested but the one service from me – to be landed on the coast of France at a certain place and on a certain date. Not a service altogether easy to fulfil, but one which I shall provide in the fullest degree. *Implacable*, seventy-four – one of the very few available, Lord Melcombe – will be placed at Baron de Kolli's disposal. Captain Cockburn will receive orders to take him and Don Felicito on board and land them when and where they wish – Wait!' he snapped again as Lord Melcombe attempted to speak. 'Captain

Cockburn has another and smaller vessel in his command. A schooner, Mr Croker, is it not?'

'Schooner *Nonpareil*, my lord,' Croker answered briskly.

'Just so. The Spaniards will transfer to the schooner, who can come closer in to the coast, and will be landed from her. The seventy-four will keep her station at a rendezvous, signals and so forth to be arranged, for the purpose of taking off De Kolli if his mission proves successful. I fail to see –'

'That's the *if*!' Melcombe, banging a hand on the table, had lost his diffidence. 'Your pardon, my lord, but 'twasn't your arrangements I was doubting but the Spaniards'. I can't see the mission succeeding with De Kolli in charge of it.'

'Oh come now, my lord,' said Croker. 'The Baron's shrewd enough, if something of a windbag. And the other, Maura, spoke sense whenever he opened his mouth.'

'Which wasn't often, Mr Croker,' said Melcombe, shaking his head. 'De Kolli's the leader. And what's he setting out to do?' He turned to the Foreign Secretary. 'See here, my lord. You'll land 'em on the Biscay coast – I don't doubt you can do it, and secretly. But what then? They make for Valençay. I know where that is, and it's a good fifty leagues from the coast, a hundred and fifty miles inside Bonaparte's France. Then they've to get fifty leagues back again, with –'

'This is useless, Lord Melcombe,' Wellesley said wearily. 'You heard the Baron's account of the aid he is to receive and the plans that have been made, of the secret exchange of messages, of the safe refuges he will find. You speak of Bonaparte's France, but behind the Biscay coast is a France that is still largely anti-Republican.'

'Chouans north of the Loire and Vendéans south of it,' put in Croker.

'Just so. My own agents have reported as much. I have no reason to doubt De Kolli's arrangements, nor should Lord Melcombe have.'

'After all,' Croker said persuasively, 'it's only six years since Cadoudal and Pichegru and their men struck at Bonaparte.'

'Cadoudal and Pichegru ended on the guillotine,' Melcombe said, but less confidently.

'And the armies they'd raised went to ground.' The Navy secretary leaned across the table. 'Thousands of men, my lord, in Brittany and Poitou – farmers and peasants, I grant you, but all ready to speed another blow at the Corsican. For that's what this mission will be.'

The Marquess, with a keen glance at the old man's still doubtful countenance, spoke with less acerbity than before.

'The plan is indeed a daring one, as you have perceived, my lord. There must, as you remarked, be chances and hazards. But even against these it could succeed.'

'It could succeed,' Croker repeated, sitting back and considering his fingernails thoughtfully.

'Aye – I dare say, I dare say.' Melcombe looked unhappily from one to the other of them. 'So I'm to inform His Majesty you'll land 'em and leave 'em. He won't like it, I can tell you. See here, now. A moment ago you spoke of agents, British agents on French soil, as I take it. Why couldn't –'

'By God!' Croker broke in, sitting up suddenly. 'You've hit it, my lord. We should have thought of that.' He faced the Foreign Secretary. 'Verlay's the man for it, and he's in London now. He reported at the Admiralty yesterday.'

'Verlay?' Wellesley repeated, looking hard at him.

'Francis Verlay. Pitt's best agent, knows southern France like the back of his hand, could be most useful to De Kolli and Maura. I suggest your lordship sends for him.'

Lord Melcombe's heavy face brightened. 'I know the name,' he said with animation. 'I've heard Mr Pitt himself – God rest his soul! – mention this Verlay. "Worth an army corps to us," was what he said. Dammit, if you send Verlay with 'em –'

'I shall see Mr Verlay as soon as he can be brought here,' Wellesley said with sudden decision. 'He will be given an exact briefing and the Spanish envoys will be confided to his care. We shall then, I think, have done the utmost in our power. You agree, I trust?' he added with a touch of sarcasm.

'Oh, I agree. It's the King I have to satisfy, y' know.'

'And His Majesty, you think, will be content with our arrangements as they now stand?'

'I believe so, I believe so.' Lord Melcombe heaved himself laboriously to his feet. 'I can see him before he takes his noon draught if I leave now. You'll excuse me, gentlemen?'

When the door had closed behind the King's confidant Wellesley turned a frowning stare on Croker.

'Have we time?' he demanded.

'Certainly. *Implacable* sails on seventh September and today's the third. Verlay can leave tonight – and it'll be safer if our Spaniards know nothing about him. The udmost zegrezy, you know,' Croker added with a grin.

'And you think this necessary?'

'I do, my lord. Something – a little – was being left to chance. By using Verlay we ensure success.'

The Foreign Secretary drew a sheet of paper towards him and dipped his quill in the inkwell.

' "'Tis not in mortals to command success," ' he quoted gravely, ' "But we'll do more – deserve it." '

Croker laughed.

2

Lieutenant Robert Ring, commanding His Majesty's armed schooner *Nonpareil*, was in his cabin writing up the ship's Log. It was not an easy task. The schooner was heeled well over with a stiff breeze on her starboard beam, so that Ring's white breeches slithered about on the polished oak lid of the sea-chest he was sitting on and the log-book tended to slide down the slope of the little table, which was hinged to the bulkhead. The sea-chest, the table, and the truckle-bed just about filled the tiny cabin. Such light as there was came through the spaces above and below the door giving onto the alley below the companionway, and so did the gusty draughts that puffed round Ring's legs. Noise filled the cabin – the ceaseless keening of wind in the rigging, the groan of timbers, the rasp of telescope and boat-cloak swinging from a hook on the bulkhead, and the clink of platter and wineglass in the rack where he had put them after taking his noon bever. Ring was quite unconscious of the noise; *Nonpareil* had been patrolling for six weeks in these northern Biscay waters and the perpetual westerlies had rarely given him a quiet cabin or an even keel. With his left fist grasping the inkpot and clamping the book to the slanting table he dipped quill and began to write.

Tuesday 5th September 1810. A.M.Ile de Groix N by E 15 miles.

Exercised gun crews. Wind WSW fresh to strong. Scrubbed hammocks.'

He stopped writing and stared at the last two words. *Scrubbed hammocks.* They were a kind of symbol of his sea life over the past year-and-a-half: dull routine, running messages for *Implacable*, cruising up and down an enemy coast with never an action with the enemy. When he had left the *Montagu* 74 to take over *Nonpareil* – and with her the courtesy rank of captain – he had, it seemed, exchanged the continual possibility of action for the probability of none. To Robert Ring, still a lieutenant after sixteen years in the Navy, this meant that the prospect of promotion was remote indeed. But it was not so much the dwindling chance of gaining a step in rank as the dreary monotony of blockade duty that irked Ring, for he had a yearning for adventurous action that would have better befitted a featherbrained midshipman than an experienced sea-officer of thirty.

Ring's uncomfortable thoughts brought no change of expression on his square weather-browned face. He dismissed them and returned to his log. *'Course ESE. Main, fore, and 2 jibs ...'* The quill stopped and he reflected for a moment. Abel Turfrey – by rights the man should be logged for fighting in the mess-deck. The second time, too, after being warned; Ring had stopped his rum issue for a week. But he was well aware that Turfrey was under strong provocation, being the only landsman in the schooner's little crew of twenty men. He had joined at Plymouth six weeks ago, one of three men supplied by the port admiral to make up his deficiency. The other two were seamen of a sort but Turfrey was a yokel who had been gaoled for poaching, a sea ignoramus who was bound to be the butt of the others.

Ring felt a certain sympathy for him because he had, in his time, been something of a butt himself. His mother, now dead, had been a Frenchwoman; and when it became known in the midshipman's berth that Midshipman Ring had the blood of England's enemies in his veins his life had become a round of gibes and battles. Yes, excuses might be found for Abel Turfrey's behaviour; but the Navy never accepted excuses. And yet the man was much above the average of pressgang recruits, a six-footer and strong as an ox, quick to learn and clever with his hands. It would take more than six weeks' service to make a seaman of him but given time –

Here Ring's meditations were interrupted by a distant screech that overtopped the sea-noises, the words indistinguishable but their portent instantly intelligible to *Nonpareil*'s captain. The lookout at the foremasthead had sighted a sail.

Since the schooner had seen no other vessel for a week, and a vessel in these waters was nearly certain to be French, her commander might have been expected to dash incontinently on deck. Robert Ring first screwed on the top of his inkpot and placed it in the locker under the deckhead together with the log-book, moving rapidly but without haste. Then he put on his cocked hat, slung the telescope on his shoulder by its strap, and climbed up through the companionway to the after-deck.

Breckinridge met him as he came up. 'Sail to windward, sir,' he clamoured excitedly, forestalling inquiry. 'Eight miles or more on the beam and same course as us. Lookout reckons she's a French *chasse-marée*, sir.'

Breckinridge was Ring's second-in-command, a junior lieutenant of six months' standing and ten years younger than Ring. In contrast with his captain, who was of the middle height and broad-shouldered, he was tall and thin.

'Very well, Mr Breckinridge,' Ring said. 'I'll have a look at her.'

As he spoke his glance took in the twenty-five yards of tilted deck reaching for'ard to the long bowsprit: the boats on their chocks amidships, the guns – two on either side – in their spray-covers, the half-dozen men of the watch-on-deck squatting below the weather rail with their faces turned towards him expectantly. The man at the wheel beside him was Abel Turfrey, taking his spell while Lunt the boatswain kept a watchful eye on him; he was glad to note that his arrival on deck didn't distract Turfrey's attention from his steering for a moment. He stepped to the shrouds and climbed steadily up to the mainmasthead, where the narrow platform was ringed to the topmast. The topmast was bare, for he hadn't hoisted gaff-topsail or staysail, and he had an excellent view all round.

'She's yarnder, sir – right abeam!' yelled the lookout on the foremasthead forty feet away, unnecessarily.

Ring braced his back against the topmast and steadied his telescope. The day was clear under the high grey overcast and the vast heaving plain of sea, grey-green flecked with white, stretched to the dark rim of horizon. The white speck almost on the horizon jumped into focus in the telescope's circle. A small vessel; two masts, square sails on both, with single jib for'ard and jigger aft; a *chasse-marée* beyond a doubt, and on a converging rather than a parallel course to *Nonpareil*'s. She might have got out of Brest, dodging Home Popham's blockading squadron, but it was more likely she was out of one of the smaller ports south of the Penmarch. Her present course could be for Quiberon Bay or farther down the coast to the Loire mouth and Nantes. Whatever her mission, she had seized the right opportunity for it, for by now it must be known in every port on the south Breton coast that the British 74 that for more than a year had threatened all coastal traffic had left her station. With her eight guns and crew of thirty or forty men a *chasse-marée* could ignore the presence of a 75-ton schooner armed with four guns. Or so she might think.

Ring lowered his telescope and turned to glance across the empty sea to eastward. Beyond that horizon was the French coast, a dozen miles away. Ahead, beyond the curve of *Nonpareil*'s big foresail, lay the Teignouse Passage into Quiberon Bay, between Belle-Ile and the Quiberon peninsula; in half-an-hour or less he expected to sight the Poulains point on Belle-Ile, and when he did so he had reached the southern terminus of his patrol. He had a weighty decision to make and not much time in which to make it.

Implacable, with *Nonpareil* as auxiliary, had been assigned the duty of watching over the coastal waters between the Pointe de Penmarch and Quiberon Bay. At Brest and Rochefort the big ships of the French fleet were penned in by blockading British squadrons, keeping the seas clear for the vital supply-lines to Wellington's army in Spain. Since the Breton ports harboured only a few small armed vessels and it was known that no French ships-of-the-line were in Quiberon Bay, a single 74 had been deemed adequate for this service. But *Implacable*, an old ship, had lost half her upper spars in a freak squall at the end of August, and having used up her spares during the previous winter had had to return to Plymouth for re-rigging. Captain Cockburn had named 9th September for their rendezvous at his usual station ten miles south-west of the Penmarch and had left no orders beyond the patrolling course *Nonpareil* was to follow during his absence. The schooner was not designed to engage in a sea-fight; her duties were to observe and report, to carry dispatches, to chase venturous coasting vessels back into port. It was no business of hers to bring about a single-ship action in the frigate tradition. All the same –

Robert Ring was aware, at the back of his mind, that his decision had been taken even before he put his telescope to his eye, but – characteristically – he had to find himself good reasons for it; they had to be good, to set against the cold fact that he intended to engage an enemy vessel of twice his own strength. First, then, the French must be shown that their coasts were firmly blockaded, *Implacable* or no *Implacable*. (That, surely, was his plain duty.) Second, his crew were bored and discontented – the recent trouble in the mess-deck showed that – and nothing could be better as a remedy than a fight against odds. And third, he would never forgive himself for the rest of his life if he refused to accept a challenge.

For challenge it was. A final glance through the telescope showed him the *chasse marée*, larger now in the lens, holding steadily on her course; a course which would cross his bows, for with her greater spread of sail she was fore-reaching on the schooner. She must have seen and recognised *Nonpareil*, and was completely ignoring her. If a fourth reason had been needed that would do.

He slung the telescope and stepped down onto the ratlines. Below him on the long narrow deck, with the white foam streaming away astern, his whole ship's company stood with their faces upturned to him; from vertically above they looked like clusters of pink lozenges. Ring smiled, a rare thing with him. He knew them all well enough to know that every man there was hoping for the decision he'd made.

'Hands to make sail, Mr Breckinridge,' he said briskly as his foot touched the deck. 'Tops'l, stays'l, flying jib.' Breckinridge sprang for'ard shouting and he turned to the boatswain. 'We'll have the spray-covers off the guns, Mr Lunt.'

'Aye, aye, sir,' said Lunt; he was a stocky elderly man, nearly bald. 'Load an' run out, sir?'

Ring paused for the fraction of a second before replying. 'Yes. And send Buller aft to take over the helm.'

As Lunt trotted away a deep voice spoke unexpectedly at Ring's elbow.

'So please ye, sir, I could handle her – got the feel of her now, I have,' said Turfrey.

Ring whirled to face him, 'Question my orders again and you'll feel the cat,' he snapped; and then, remembering the man's inexperience, 'Are you the best helmsman aboard this vessel?'

Turfrey, abashed, tugged at the yellow forelock that overhung his craggy features. 'Beg parding, sir,' he mumbled. 'No, sir, I ain't – not yet.'

'Well, Buller is.' Buller came running aft as he spoke. 'As she goes, Buller.'

'As she goes, sir,' said Buller, grasping the spokes and shouldering the other man out of the way.

Ring watched Turfrey loping for'ard, his gaunt figure lurching in unseamanlike fashion, to join the little crowd of men busy round the guns; but his mind was on other matters. If the Frenchman held on his slowly converging course it was a little early to clear for action, but there was always the possibility that the *chasse-marée* might decide to attack, coming down on him from windward. His own plan – it had been formed as soon as he saw her – had visualized a running fight, which would enable him to use the only advantage he possessed. It was a hundred to one that the *chasse-marée* followed the usual pattern of her class and mounted 12-pounder carronades, effective only at ranges of under half-a-mile. The schooner's long 4-pounders had a range of a mile.

Nonpareil heeled steeply and then began to move more swiftly through the water as the wind filled-out her upper sails. On a wind she would have the heels of the Frenchman, whose square sails needed a wind abaft the beam for full efficiency. That the enemy had the weather-gauge couldn't be helped at this stage and might even assist Ring's gunnery. A broadside (if you could call it that) of only two 4-pounders was going to call for skilled gunnery, and Ring could look back with satisfaction on the daily gun-drill and the twice-weekly banging away at floating casks that had given him gun-crews that were at least competent.

A gleam of white showed to starboard as the schooner rose on a ruffled wave-crest. She was closing faster than he had thought but not fore-reaching on him now. His telescope showed her clearly, holding a white bone between her teeth as she foamed along with the wind over her quarter.

'Deck, there! Land – land fine on th' stabb'd bow!'

As the hail shrilled from the masthead Breckinridge came running aft.

'That'll be Belle-Ile all guns loaded and run out cleared for action sir,' he said in a single breathe.

'I trust not, Mr Breckinridge,' Ring said solemnly.

Breckinridge grinned briefly. 'Our guns, I mean – and she's heading in for the Teignouse, sir, sure as houses.'

'Yes. Come below – Mr Lunt! Take the deck for a moment. And hoist our colours, if you please.'

The chart, spread between them on the cabin table, had little to tell them that they didn't know already, for *Nonpareil* had twice made a reconnaissance into Quiberon Bay; but there would be no time to consult charts once the action had begun. Breckinridge, who prided himself on his pilotage, ran his forefinger across the marked soundings with a jerky and unnecessary commentary. The 11-mile length of Belle-Ile guarding the entrance on the south; the long flat peninsula of Quiberon on the north stretching its subtended line of islands and rocks like a rank of sentries; between Houat island and Quiberon was the only passage for a vessel of any size, and that was considerably narrowed by the great rock of the Teignouse itself. At high water there was a bare two miles of sea-room in the Teignouse Passage.

'Tide?' Ring demanded, rolling the chart and dropping it into the rack.

'Slack water of the flood in one hour, sir.'

On Breckinridge's words came the hail from the masthead again – land, on the port bow this time.

'You'll sail her,' Ring threw over his shoulder as they climbed to the deck. 'I'll take the guns.'

'Aye aye, sir.'

The *chasse-marée* was in full view from the deck now, on the same course and converging fast. Beyond the bowsprit and its three straining jibs Ring could see the dark outline of Belle-Ile on the horizon almost ahead, and when the schooner lifted on the crest of the long Atlantic rollers he caught a glimpse of the Quiberon peninsula, flat as a raft on the port bow. The two ships were racing for the wide gap between the two; wide in appearance but narrowed by the chain of rocks reaching north-west from Houat towards the Teignouse rock off Quiberon's southern point. In a few minutes he was able to perceive that the French ship would enter the passage before *Nonpareil*, though she was (he thought) making slightly less speed.

'Steer to bring her on the beam and five cables distant,' he told Breckinridge.

Five cables, rather more than half-a-mile, was well within the limit of his long fours but near extreme range for carronades. If only she held her course her possession of the weather-gauge could be a positive disadvantage to the *chasse-marée* in the gunnery duel he was hoping for. And she held on, scudding into the entrance two miles clear of the Poulains point and barely a mile to starboard of the schooner. Perhaps, thought Ring, her mission was so urgent that she couldn't risk stopping to fight; at any rate, she evidently believed she could outdistance *Nonpareil*. He ran his eye over the sails – fore and main drawing well with their long booms far out over the port rail, the square foretopsail showing too much bag. Half-a-dozen hands jumped to sheets and braces at his shout and the foretopsail was hauled into full efficiency. The schooner, hitherto slightly astern on her parallel course, began slowly to draw level.

Ring nodded to Breckinridge beside the wheel and went for'ard. All four of his guns were for'ard of midships and the dozen men who manned them were standing ready, matches smouldering in the nicks on the rims of the water-casks. A 4-pounder needed a gun-crew of five so he could only man two guns at a time, with two reserves standing by the inactive guns.

'Starboard gun-captains, you'll fire on my word,' he said. 'Layers, adjust for low elevation. Now – train on her mainmast.'

He reached a hand to the foreshrouds and sprang up to balance himself on the starboard rail. The *chasse-marée* was almost abeam now, and so close that he could see the dark clusters of men on her tilted deck; like the schooner, she was steeply heeled to port, and her gunports were almost hidden by the white waves racing along her side. Beyond her a distant spout of white caught his eye – the rocks off Houat island – and beyond that was the coast of Belle-Ile fast dwindling astern. Turning, he saw the brief upsurge of foam that marked the Teignouse rock half-a-mile away on his port hand. Yes; easy enough to slip through the Teignouse Passage on a flood tide in fair weather, but possibly not so easy to beat back through it. He was entering Quiberon Bay with its deeply-indented rocky coasts, *côtes sauvages* as the Bretons called them, under his lee. A lee shore was a hazard in any case, but this one was an enemy shore too, and doubly dangerous. And now the *chasse-marée* was dead abeam.

'Gun-captains mark your target,' he said briskly. 'Stand by.'

He gauged the angle of the schooner's side below him, its changing tilt as a long wave passed under her.

'Number two gun – fire!'

The 4-pounder flamed and roared and lurched back on the relieving-tackles. Above the grey cloud-ceiling the sun was westering, and Ring shaded his eyes against the pallid light to see the fall of shot. A momentary plume of white rose just short of the Frenchman but dead in line. He waited and gauged again.

'Number four – fire!'

No fall of shot to be seen. Over, probably. Number two had reloaded and they were running the gun out, Turfrey's angular figure among the men hauling on the ropes. The ragged crash of the Frenchman's guns came loudly down the wind but there was no sign of the shot; heeled at that angle it was likely the balls hadn't travelled more than fifty fathoms before striking the surface.

'Number two – fire!'

Again, no fall of shot to be seen, but an excited yell from Breckinridge sharpened his gaze and he saw that the *chasse-marée*'s main-shrouds had parted.

'Well done, men – Number four – fire!'

Short, but only by a few fathoms. And here came the Frenchman's second broadside. He'd contrived to get extra elevation on his carronades, for spouts of water rose a pistol-shot from *Nonpareil*'s side, but it wasn't likely he'd do better than that. Which was just as well, for the schooner's thin planking was easy prey for 12-pounder balls. If Ring had been the French captain, he told himself, he'd have closed the range before this. And, precisely as number two gun fired, the *chasse-marée* put her helm down.

The instant she began to turn Ring sprang down beside number four gun, which had just reloaded.

'Handspikes here – look lively!'

Nonpareil was just starting to forereach. He trained the gun, stooped to peer through the port along the gun-barrel, and shouted as he sprang aside.

'Fire!'

The 4-pounder flashed and lurched back. The French ship, almost bows-on and not more than three cables away, seemed to be taking on a list. But it was the stricken mast, the mainmast with its two huge sails, that was leaning away from its severed shrouds to collapse in a great flurry of canvas and cordage that smothered half the deck and trailed overside, swinging the *chasse-marée* broadside-on again.

Ring's shout cut short the hoarse cheers of the gun-crews.

'Stand to your guns – she's not finished yet! Independent fire, and see that you aim –'

There was a splintering crash and the schooner's hull shuddered. Ring felt the wind of a 12-pounder ball as it hummed past his ear. It was chance that had swung the Frenchman so that his starboard guns were bearing and he'd made the most of it; chance again – and again in the enemy's favour – that Breckinridge had chosen that moment, immediately after Ring's successful shot, to put his helm down and bring *Nonpareil* round to starboard so that her guns would continue to bear, thus causing her to heel and expose more of her side. Ring, as he roared orders for sail to be taken in, was wondering whether she had been hit on or below the waterline.

The two ships were closing rapidly now. On the deck of the *chasse-marée* they were working frantically to clear the wreckage, but the trailing mast and gear prevented her from answering the helm and her guns would no longer bear. *Nonpareil*'s two guns banged in succession once and again as, under reduced sail, she slowly approached her helpless opponent. Splinters flew from the Frenchman's rail; a man screamed.

'Lay alongside, Mr Breckinridge!' Ring yelled. 'Stand by to board, you men!'

This, as he well knew, was not the wisest of decisions; his men would be outnumbered by at least two to one in the hand-to-hand fighting, and it would have been safer to stand off and pound her into submission. It was Ring's foible that he hated abandoning the momentum of direct attack. Perhaps fortunately, the *chasse-marée* gave him no opportunity of boarding, for she hauled down her colours amid the triumphant screeching of *Nonpareil*'s men. The schooner came to the wind and lay hove-to two cables from her victim.

'Away longboat's crew! – Mr Breckinridge, aboard with you and take possession. Six men, pistols and cutlasses. Send her captain over to me.' Ring turned to the gun-crews. 'Keep those guns trained on her, d'ye hear?'

He walked aft, well pleased with himself and his crew. *Nonpareil* had a prize at last, and without so much as a scratch among her people. It would be a problem to man her, though, and the business of rigging a jury-mast and getting her out through the Teignouse Passage would have to be started without delay; the saffron glow in the grey sky heralded sunset and the ebb had already begun. He would put the Frenchmen into their boats and they'd have a four-mile pull to the Morbihan coast – it was just in sight on the eastern horizon. If there were any wounded among them he'd have to take them on board –

'Sirr!'

Norie, ship's carpenter, confronted him with the boatswain beside him. Norie's wizened face was screwed into a worried scowl.

'We're making water right fast,' he said rapidly. 'Yon felly lappit us half-a-fathom below water-line, and I canna get at it.'

'Very well, Mr Norie. Mr Lunt, rig the pump and get to work, quick as you can.'

'I doot the pump will suffeece, sir,' said Norie as Lunt hurried away. 'In my judgement we may need to fother her.'

'We'll try the pump first,' Ring nodded.

His face as he turned to stand at the rail showed nothing of his sudden anxiety. The longboat with Breckinridge and his boarding-party was halfway to the *chasse-marée*, and on the horizon beyond the French ship he could see the low silhouette of an island against the dull suffusion of the sinking sun. Houat island, that must be. He was far into Quiberon Bay, at the close of day with the ebb-tide running, with a rocky and hostile shore under his lee and (it seemed likely now) an unseaworthy vessel to take out to safety. He would have no hands to spare for manning a prize.

Lunt and his party were rigging the pump. It was an unwieldy apparatus that clamped to the rail with a long leathern hose which was unrolled – with much difficulty and profanity – down the companionway. He watched the first gush spout overside as they began to pump; clear water, not the dirt of the bilges. Already *Nonpareil*'s slow roll on the swell felt sluggish under his feet.

'Mr Lunt!' he called suddenly. 'Rouse out the spare mains'l and have it rigged ready for fothering.'

As he spoke he saw the longboat heading back to the schooner, and two minutes later Breckinridge arrived panting on the after-deck.

'No trouble, sir,' Breckinridge said breathlessly. 'All under hatches for the time being, with a guard on 'em. Went like lambs. She's the *Faucon*, out of Camaret, eight guns and crew of thirty-four.'

'And this is her captain?'

Ring was eyeing the man who had followed his lieutenant on board, a lean gentleman, very erect in blue civilian coat and elegant drabs with a low-crowned round hat in the latest mode.

'No, sir,' said Breckinridge. 'Her captain and one seaman were killed by our last shot. This is some sort of passenger. Anxious to talk to you, far as I can gather – me not speaking the lingo. Name's Labby, or something like it.'

'Labiche, François Labiche,' said the passenger, stepping forward. '*M. le capitaine, je voudrais quelques minutes de conversation.*' He glanced briefly at Breckingridge. '*Un peu plus de réclusion, peut-être. Vous avez compris?*' he added.

'*Parfaitement,*' Ring answered; he hesitated for a moment. '*Allons en bas. Précédez-moi, monsieur, je vous en prie.*'

He indicated the companionway and followed Labiche down the ladder. In the dark little cabin Ring sat on the truckle-bed and his visitor on the sea-chest facing him. Ring

waited for the other man to speak first and in the short pause
the grunts of the men at the pump and the rhythmic splash of
water overside sounded loud. When Labiche spoke it was,
unexpectedly, in English.

'My dear fellow,' he drawled, eyeing Ring with his head on
one side, 'I do congratulate you on your French. Not a trace of
accent – quite incredible.'

Ring concealed his surprise. 'I might say the same of your
English, monsieur,' he returned evenly.

'Ah, but our cases are dissimilar, captain. You are not a
Frenchman, but I am an Englishman. I was christened Francis
Verlay, and I am an agent of His Britannic Majesty's
government.'

3

The dim light in the cabin revealed only the salient points of
the self-styled agent's features: high cheekbones side-
whiskered, a high-bridged nose, eyes narrowed and bright.
There had been a kind of arrogant complacency in his
statement that annoyed Ring.

'A spy,' he said, not troubling to conceal his distaste.

The other shrugged. 'I fight against Bonaparte, as you do.
With this difference, captain. If you are taken you're treated
like a gentleman and exchanged. If I'm taken I'm first tortured
and then shot. You, I fancy, are hardly in a position to judge
the relative merit of our services.'

Ring let that pass. 'How do you come to be on board a
French vessel of war?'

'By virtue of this.' Verlay took a thin leather wallet from his
pocket and pushed it across the table. 'Monsieur Labiche was –
and, in my person, still is – one of the Emperor's most trusted
and authoritative agents of secret police. Monsieur Labiche
arrived in Roscoff, ostensibly from Rennes but in reality from
London, and travelled post overland to Crozon, where he
demanded from the *maire* immediate and speedy transport to
Nantes, in the Emperor's name. A *chasse-marée* chanced to be in
the harbour at Camaret five miles from Crozon.' He spread his
hands. '*C'est tout.*'

Ring was peering at the parchment-like paper that was sewn to the fold of the wallet. It bore a dozen lines of writing ending in an indecipherable signature and a gold seal with a crown on it.

'The description here, of François Labiche, seems to fit you very well, Mr Verlay,' he remarked.

'That was unfortunate for François Labiche, captain,' Verlay said, 'as was his habit of working alone. He – died, very inconspicuously, three weeks ago.'

'And you can impose on the French authorities with this?' Ring demanded incredulously, handing back the wallet.

'For another three weeks, perhaps. Then the *bureau* in Paris will begin to wonder why M. Labiche has not reported.' Verlay stowed the wallet in an inner pocket and leaned forward. 'To the point, now. I am engaged upon an urgent mission on the orders of the Marquess Wellesley. You have interrupted it – oh, I don't blame you, my dear fellow – and I require you to rectify the interruption.'

'I've seen no authority but that of Bonaparte, Mr – Verlay.'

'Do you expect me to carry papers from the Foreign Secretary?' Verlay snapped impatiently. 'Listen. When did you last visit the Admiralty, captain?'

'Six weeks ago.'

'Doubtless you went to the Pay Office. You turned to the right at the top of a stairway, passing a framed daub purporting to represent the Glorious First of June. You entered the second door on the left. You stated your name, substantive rank, and ship to an aged dotard with a face like a rotting apple. Well?'

Ring nodded briefly. 'What do you want me to do?'

'Obviously the *chasse-marée* cannot take me to Nantes, nor can you. I require you, therefore, to set me ashore on the coast between the Croisic and St Nazaire, under cover of darkness, and without delay. You have no more than four leagues to cover, and with this wind –'

'It's impossible,' Ring cut in with decision.

'I demand it in the King's name!' Verlay cried angrily. 'If you're afraid for your precious prize-money –'

'Damn your impertinence!' Ring swallowed his temper. 'See here, Mr Verlay. His Majesty's name can't make my ship seaworthy. She's holed below the waterline and my work's cut out to keep her afloat, let alone sail her to Le Croisic.'

Verlay scowled at him in silence for a moment. 'Very well. You carry a longboat and a cockboat, I see. You can get sail on your longboat and land me at the nearest point –'

There was a bang on the door and Breckinridge put his head into the cabin.

'Your pardon, sir,' he said worriedly, 'but the pump's not gaining. She's down a bit by the head already.'

'Very well. I'll come on deck. Tell the boatswain to look sharp with the fothering sail – and Mr Breckinridge!' he added as the lieutenant withdrew. 'Are there any wounded aboard the Frenchman?'

'No, sir. Just the two dead.'

Ring faced the secret agent. 'You heard that. I can spare neither boat nor men.'

'It is your duty to put me ashore!' Verlay said in a rage. 'By virtue of the authority vested in me by the Marquess Wellesley I order you to do so!'

'I know my duty, thank you.' Ring stood up, bending his head below the deckhead beams. 'It's to my ship. I take my orders from the Admiralty. The Marquess Wellesley can go hang.' He waved a hand to the door. 'On deck, if you please.'

'You'll hear more of this, captain,' Verlay said between his teeth as he went out.

'I'm sending *Faucon*'s people ashore in their own boats,' Ring said, mounting the companion-ladder behind him. 'You'll go with them, Mr Verlay – Mr Breckinridge, take Monsieur Labiche back to his ship, if you please. Have her boats launched and see that every man aboard embarks. When they're well clear, set fire to the ship and return on board.'

'Set fire –? Aye aye, sir,' said Breckinridge; he was unable to keep the disappointment from his voice.

Verlay climbed down into the longboat without another word, his lean face grimly set. Ring watched it pull away towards the *chasse-marée*. The wind had fallen away and the slight splashes as the oars dipped were the only flecks of white on the long dark swell. Daylight was fast fading behind the grey west and Houat island showed a small black bar on the darkening horizon. Beside him the pump hurled its succession of brief torrents overboard.

'Ready for fothering, sir,' said Lunt at his elbow.

He turned and went for'ard with the boatswain. The spare sail, smeared with tar and oakum, had to be got under the bows and then drawn aft along the hull below water, in the hope that the inrush of water would suck it against the shot-hole and stop the worst of the leakage. When he had seen the operation well under way, with the difficult business of coaxing the fothering sail into place begun, Ring looked again at the *chasse-marée*. Breckinridge and his six men in the longboat were nearing the schooner; much farther away and to southward he could just make out the three black specks of the boats heading towards the French coast. Ring spared a moment to wonder what sort of mission Mr Francis Verlay had undertaken for the British government, and how Monsieur Labiche had explained to his temporary compatriots his visit to *Nonpareil*. Then his attention was caught by the thin red flame that licked suddenly upwards abaft the French ship's fallen mast. The mass of canvas caught fire and went up in a great yellow glare.

'Longboat hoisting aboard, sir,' said Breckinridge behind him. 'They'll see that blaze on the mainland,' he added.

Ring nodded. There might be gunboats in the little harbours over there, Port Navalo and Quiberon and Auray. *Nonpareil* was in no state to cope with gunboats.

'We'll get under way, Mr Breckinridge,' he said; then, remembering that the blaze had put paid to his lieutenant's hopes of prize-money, 'There was no alternative. We're likely to need every hand we've got.'

'I understand, sir. Thank you,' said Breckinridge. 'What course to steer, sir?'

'West by south.'

There was no uncertainty in Ring's voice. Here, too, there was no alternative.

Five minutes later *Nonpareil* crept away in the deepening twilight, her pump still frantically at work. Astern of her she left a smouldering wreck from which at irregular intervals came the flash and report of exploding ammunition. Within her sluggishly-rolling hull the sea-water swilled, spurting up here and there through the seams of the mess-deck planking.

II

Houat Island

1

'Deep six ... deep six ... by the mark five ...'

The leadsman's voice came aft to where Ring stood beside the helm. *Nonpareil* was groping her way through the gathering darkness towards the land, rolling slowly and heavily on the swell; like a portly alderman, he thought, with his belly full of port and conscious of the need for care. The schooner's belly was half-full of seawater, for the fothering of her wounded side had done no more than make it possible for the pump to hold its own against the inrush of water. The black outline of the land was less than a mile ahead now and giving a lee, so that the westerly had dropped to a light breeze.

'By the mark five ... by the mark five ... less a quarter ...'

Shallowing very slowly. And the ebb had begun an hour ago. The leadsman's next call gave five fathoms again. That was Abel Turfrey's deep voice; a voice more suggestive of thickets and copses than of shipboard. Ring could just see his gaunt figure balancing on the lee rail for'ard as he whirled the lead-line for his next cast. He had instructed Turfrey in taking soundings on *Nonpareil*'s last cruise into Quiberon Bay, discovering that the one-time poacher had a ready grasp of any physical knack and never needed to be told anything twice. On that last cruise, too, he had taken the schooner close in to Houat for a reconnaissance of the north coast of the island; he had reason now to bless that reconnaissance.

From the moment *Nonpareil*'s plight became apparent Ring had known that Houat was her only hope. The gaping shot-hole below her waterline could be repaired; he carried materials enough, and with the planking well battened inboard and a copper tingle applied outboard Norie could have her sound again in twelve hours. But to do this she must be careened, high and dry on a beach, so that the water could be pumped out of her for the carpenter to work. Houat, the nearest land, was also the one place where he had a chance of doing this.

The island was a mere sliver of grass-topped rock a mile long and a quarter-mile wide, nowhere rising more than a hundred feet above the sea. Until five years ago the French had maintained a small fort on its western tip fronting the Teignouse Passage, but this was half-ruinous now, though there were still a few fishermen living in the tiny hamlet perched above an inlet at the eastern end of Houat; he had seen through his telescope the smoke rising from their fires, and the masts of half-a-dozen small craft at the stone jetty below. The telescope had also shown him the sandy beaches between the hamlet and the ruined fort. On the south Houat fronted the Atlantic with rocks and reefs, but here on the side facing inward to the mainland five miles away were long stretches of sand with gentle hillocks behind them. Towards the most westerly of these beaches he was steering now.

Half-a-mile to go. The black outline rose higher ahead and the blocks rattled in a fitful wind. Breckinridge ran aft from his post in the bows.

'Light on the port beam, sir,' he said. 'Leastways, there was – it's gone now. Must've been in a boat, though.'

'Night-fishing, like as not,' Ring said. 'Hands to fore and main halyards, Mr Breckinridge, and stand by to down sail. Mr Lunt, check that all's fast below decks.'

Lunt's dark figure disappeared down the companionway. Breckinridge, who had begun to trot for'ard, slid to a halt with a shout, pointing over the rail to port.

'Boat, sir – closing us!'

Ring saw the big lugsail first, then the boat, a broad-beamed half-decked craft the size of his longboat. A hail came from her.

'*Quel vaisseau, là?*'

The voice, high and full, was like a woman's. The boat luffed-up and held a parallel course a biscuit-toss away.

'*Faucon*, Camaret,' Ring shouted back at random; he needed all his attention for his course.

'*Menteur, vous!*' returned the voice scornfully. '*Faucon est chasse-marée.*'

It added something more, but Ring shouted it down impatiently, in French. 'My ship is sinking and I am going to beach her. Keep clear!'

Throughout this brief exchange his ear had been tuned to the leadsman's chant. 'By the mark three,' it was now. He had less than six feet of water under his keel. The next minute or two were going to be ticklish work, for he wanted to take her as far up the beach as he could and yet must ground her gently if he was to keep his masts standing.

'Halyards, there! Down fore and main!'

The sails flapped and cracked as the yards were lowered. *Nonpareil* began to lose way rapidly. Ahead the pale glimmer of the beach above the tidemark, to starboard a low black line of rocks marking the western extremity of the beach.

'Three less a half,' came Turfrey's voice.

The lead-line whistled as he swung it for the next cast and then she grounded with a shock that shook her timbers and brought a groan from stays and shrouds. It was done, and well done. The schooner had brought up all standing not fifty yards short of the white glimmer where the surf, a very slight one, broke along the beach.

Ring's orders had been given and his dispositions on board made while it was still light enough to see. In a surprisingly short space of time the cockboat was pulling inshore to lay out the anchor, Breckinridge and Lunt were supervising the transfer of the starboard 4-pounders to the port side (this was to ensure that she would lie over to that side when the tide left her) and the longboat was on its way to the beach with Ring himself and six hands armed with musket and cutlass. Ring posted his sentries in a semicircle well up the beach; the odds were against any hostile demonstration by the Houat fishermen, but with *Nonpareil* immobilised and unable to use her guns it would be folly to gamble on that chance.

Standing on the rim of the receding tide, he ran his eyes slowly round the shadowy scene: the low crest above the beach rising black against the darkening sky, the bulk of a headland along the shore to eastward, the dark sea almost unnaturally calm in this sheltered place. His glance came to rest on the boat that lay aground a hundred paces along the beach, just below the surge and wallow of the little waves. Its occupant had waded ashore and was walking towards him along the sliding edge of foam. This was the fisherman who had hailed him and called him a liar, no doubt. He folded his arms and stood waiting.

The fisherman approached with short quick paces that were rendered somewhat ungainly by heavy seaboots. There was not enough light to distinguish details, and not until the dark figure was almost up to him did he perceive that it was a woman. She halted in front of him and spoke without a trace of diffidence.

'*Bon soir, M. le capitaine de vaisseau. Soyez le bienvenue à Houat.*'

She spoke, he thought as he collected his wits, as if she owned the island. But this was clearly no fisher-girl, and he lifted his hat and bowed stiffly.

'*Bon soir, mademoiselle, et bonmerci.*'

She laughed softly. '*Ah, pardon, monsieur – on ne peut pas faire une révérence en pantalons.*'

She was indeed wearing loose canvas trousers tucked into the seaboot-tops (Ring, a conventionalist, was a trifle shocked) and her small erect figure, stocky rather than slim, seemed to be clad in a thick woollen jacket and a cap like a Breton fisherman's. In the darkness he could see only that her face was round and not unattractive.

'You are an Englishman and that is an English warship,' she went on, in the Breton-accented French that reminded him of his mother's speech. 'But you need have no fear, monsieur – on Houat there are no Bonapartists. We heard the guns and saw a fire to north-eastward. You will tell me what happened, if you please.'

There was a directness about her that removed the remnants of doubt from Ring's mind. Briefly, for he wanted to get back to *Nonpareil*, he described the fight with the *chasse-marée* and the schooner's urgent need to careen and repair. She listened without interruption and then nodded approval.

'*Ça va bien.* Lying as she is your ship will float at seven tomorrow morning. But can you repair the damage overnight?'

'Certainly. We can get at the shot-hole as soon as she is

pumped dry, and my men will work by lantern-light.'

The girl shook her head doubtfully. '*Faites attention, monsieur* – lights below deck in a stranded vessel are always dangerous.'

'I shall take care, naturally,' Ring said gravely, concealing his amusement; it was a novelty to be taught his business by a girl.

'If you need materials I will ask my uncle to provide them.' She paused. 'He is the Baron de Feriet, general in the army of the Vendée.'

Ring felt slightly bewildered. Houat island was full of surprises – this extraordinary girl, a nest of anti-Bonapartists, and now a Baron-cum-General.

'I have all I need, mademoiselle, thank you,' he said. 'And now, with your leave, I must return on board my ship.'

'*Bien.* But you will visit my uncle – he will expect it.' She swung round to point at the crest above the foreshore. 'You see the dip in the skyline? Mount to that and you will find a broad path, easy to follow in the dark. Fifteen minutes of walking will bring you to the village – Port Halai is its name. Shall we say in an hour and a half?'

He found her assumption of authority irritating. The task of getting his ship afloat and away before the mainland ports came to know of her plight was a pressing one and he was in no mood for paying calls.

'It is, I think, a matter of courtesy, monsieur,' the girl added with a touch of reproach as he hesitated.

Once the job was started he could safely leave Breckinridge in charge. And the establishment of friendly relations with a French island off Quiberon could conceivably prove valuable to England.

'I will come in two hours' time, mademoiselle,' he said briefly.

She nodded. 'That will do very well. Monsieur, I do not have your name. Mine is Jeanne Bonchamps.'

'Robert Ring,' he told her.

She repeated it, giving the Christian name its French pronunciation as his mother had always done.

'Port Halai has few houses and ours is the largest,' she said. 'The path will bring you straight to it. *Alors, M. le capitaine – à bientôt.*'

'*Au 'voir, mademoiselle.*'

She turned and walked rapidly away along the beach, to splash through the shallows to where her boat showed a shifting black shape amid the surge of little waves. Peering into the obscurity, Ring watched the small dark figure, knee-deep in hurrying water, stoop to shove at the stem. The heavy craft had grounded on the fast-running ebb and for a little it seemed that the girl's efforts would never free her. He was on the point of wading in to her assistance when a last heave freed the boat. The girl scrambled aboard, the lugsail was run up, and in half-a-minute the offshore breeze had taken her away into the darkness. Mademoiselle Bonchamps, Ring reflected as he turned away, had her full share of resolution.

The sudden loom of a large body beside him made him start.

'Who's that?'

'Turfrey, sir. Beg parding, sir, but I see'd ye with the Frenchy yonder and come across to keep an eye on ye. The Frenchies is rare and handy with knives, I've heard tell.'

'Not this one, Turfrey,' Ring said, the darkness hiding his grin. 'We're among friends here, I believe. Where's your post?'

Turfrey pointed with the musket he was holding in one fist. 'Yonder, sir, 'neath the dip in they little hills. There's folks come down to the beach along that way, sir.'

'How do you know?'

'I just knows, sir.' Turfrey sounded surprised.

'Well, get back to your post. Challenge anyone who comes down to the beach, hold them there, and hail the ship. I'll send a hand to join you and you'll both be relieved at eight bells of the second dogwatch. That's less than two hours from now.'

'Aye aye, sir.'

Turfrey's odd shambling lope took him off into the darkness. Ring collected his other sentries, sent one of them to join Turfrey, and walked after the others across the wet sand to where the longboat was being kept afloat on the falling tide. Beyond her the schooner's hull and masts rose black against the paler sky; already she was lying well over to port. The pump was still discharging – he could hear the splashes – and the intermittent rasp of a carpenter's saw told that Norie was preparing his battens. By the time she was high and dry on the sand the inboard repair would be under way, but he would spell all hands for food and grog at eight bells (Breckinridge should have orders to that effect) and they could finish the work below decks before they turned in. The tingle with its underlay of fearnought could be applied outboard at first light. He would take her out through the Teignouse Passage on slack water of the flood and have ample time to reach the rendezvous appointed by Captain Cockburn.

Ring could have ordered his four men to carry him to the waiting longboat but he disliked being borne on other men's legs when his own were capable of bearing him and in any case his breeches and stockings were wet from his first landing. He was soaked to the crotch when – again disdaining help – he hauled himself into the sternsheets and took the tiller. Both he and Jeanne Bonchamps, he told himself with an inward chuckle, would have to change their trousers before their next meeting.

2

Thomas Ring, vintner of Mark Lane, had met Anne-Marie Laval during a journey to the Loire vineyards in 1779, when he had paused for some days in Redon. Pausing again on his return journey, he had married her. Anne-Marie was of the Montfort-Lavals, and Thomas had been very proud of that; he had lost no opportunity of impressing on their son that he had the best blood of Brittany in his veins. That Robert seemed indifferent to his lofty descent was something of a disappointment to his father, and later, when war was declared, the elder Ring was understandably furious when his son begged him to contradict all rumours that Midshipman Ring was half-French.

However, his mother, with whom Robert always talked and corresponded in her native language, had given him an abiding interest in Brittany and Breton affairs which was strengthened by a visit to Redon, made a few years before the Terror when Robert was boy of ten. Since then his only visits to his mother's country had been concerned with the destruction of coastal signal-stations and the blowing-up of batteries; a state of affairs that might have distressed her had she not died twelve years ago, a year after his father. But Robert had continued to interest himself in the affairs of Brittany under the Emperor Napoleon. He knew all about the 'army of the Vendée' and its tragic history, though how a general of that army was able to reside safely within a half-day's sail of the guillotine at Nantes was beyond his understanding. He was considering this and other matters as he toiled up a gully of soft sand to the crest behind the beach.

The darkness was dimly luminous, for the moon was up behind the clouds overhead. He found the path easily; broad and with ancient paving here and there, it undulated across the gently-sloping turf that ended in the drop to the shore, no doubt linking the hamlet of Port Halai to the disused fort on the western headland. Before starting along it Ring looked back to where *Nonpareil*, now lying on her side high above the retreating tide, made a dark shadow on the grey glimmer of the beach. A moving point of light winked and disappeared. Norie was already well advanced with his inboard repairs, his sentries – as he had just proved – were on the alert, and he could feel justified in leaving her for an hour or so. All the same, he was aware that he, an Englishman, was treading enemy territory alone and unarmed to enter a French village, trusting to the few words of a French girl chance-met on the beach. He felt no real qualms as to that, though. The chief impression he had received in his encounter with Jeanne Bonchamps was that here was someone to be trusted in all things.

It was a good deal windier up here than on the sheltered shore. Ring pulled his boat-cloak closer round him and settled his hat tightly on his head. The path was rising now as it rounded the brow of the little rocky cape beyond which was Port Halai, where dwelt that mysterious nobleman the Baron de Feriet.

The name De Feriet was not familiar to Ring, though he seemed to remember a Bonchamps among the rebel leaders; he recalled that there had been an undue proportion of generals in that ill-fated army of La Vendée that had opposed the Revolution in 1793 and again in 1795 when England had lent ineffective aid. Slaughter without mercy had been the lot of the insurgents then; a hopeless struggle against a swiftly-growing power. The Chouans had nevertheless risen again – eleven years ago – only to be scattered and hunted like beasts among their forests and marshes. And only six years ago their leader, Cadoudal, had headed a resolute attempt to kidnap Bonaparte in Paris itself, an enterprise that had roused the hidden adventurer in Robert Ring to ardent admiration.

Cadoudal had ended on the guillotine, like Pichegru and other Chouan leaders; but it could not be doubted that some of them – and many of the peasants who had formed their army – had escaped and were lying low. Maybe it was Napoleon's policy not to arouse the stubborn Breton spirit by further castigation. Maybe the once-dreaded signal of the Chouans, the cry of the screech-owl, would henceforward be heard only from the *chouette* itself, night-hunting in forest and *bocage*.

The path topped its rise and began to descend. Dimly seen below him on the left was the outer end of Port Halai's inlet and the jetty, soon lost to view as the path curled down to the right. Some instinct made him glance up at the crest, close above him now as he descended. A dark figure, scarcely visible against the night sky, bobbed down out of sight as his eye reached it. He walked on, dropping steeply round a bend to the left, and in a few paces saw lights close at hand. There were half-a-dozen small dwellings, single-storied, grouped just above the inlet on the hillside, but the lights were behind the curtained windows of a larger house, like an elongated barn, that stood a little higher than the others. The lit windows were the only sign of life until, as he passed below a thicket, the bushes rustled with something that was not the wind and he thought he saw a retreating shape beyond them. But the house with the lit windows was a biscuit-toss away now and the path swerved to pass its door. A shallow porch, a stout oaken door. Ring banged twice upon it with his clenched fist and at once a voice from within spoke, or rather bellowed, in response.

'*Entrez – entrez, M. l'Anglais!*'

He raised the heavy iron latch and entered a room glowing with firelight and lamplight, a room so remarkable that its peculiarities caught his attention before his glance rested on its occupant. It was a room such as he remembered seeing in

Breton farmhouses, low-beamed and narrow-windowed, with the carved wooden panels of a 'box bed' at one side; but the walls were hung with splendid tapestries, a magnificent Lebrun carpet covered the stone floor, and silver sparkled on the tops of two marquetry cabinets on either side of the big fireplace. The man who had risen from a cushioned armchair by the fire had (Ring thought) something of his room's anomaly about him, for his coat of fine broadcloth and the snowy shirt beneath it were open to display a hairy chest, and his admirable breeches terminated in bare muscular calves and feet thrust into old slippers. He was a big man inclining to corpulence, with a black moustache *au mousquetaire*. He made a formal bow and then spoke in laboured English.

'How do you, sir? Goddam well, I trust?'

Without waiting for a reply he burst into a great roar of laughter. When he laughed his large weatherbeaten face screwed itself up until the eyes were mere slits; but those eyes, Ring was aware, watched him closely.

'*Trés bien, je vous remercie, monsieur*,' he replied.

'*Ah, vous aimez mieux parler Francais – soit. Je suis nommé Yves de Feriet, M. le capitaine Ring. Et – attendez –*' De Feriet rumpled his thatch of black curls with one hand – 'please to take the bloody weight off your legs, my dee-ar fellow.'

He exploded into another guffaw as he took Ring's hat and cloak to deposit them on a table of polished walnut and placed him in a chair by the fireside opposite his own. There was an empty wineglass on a small table beside the other chair, and an empty wine-bottle on the hearth.

'No more of the English tongue, then,' De Feriet said, sitting down. 'My little Jeanne has told me you speak excellent French. As for my English, it is eleven – no, twelve years since I was in your country, seeking help for the royalists here. It was refused.'

'Refused – to General the Baron de Feriet?' said Ring, making an opportunity to confirm these titles.

De Feriet shook his head with a faint smile. 'I was not a general then. In the affair at Champtoceaux in '99, when we were defeated once and for all, I was a general – at twenty-six years of age, monsieur.'

Which makes him thirty-seven, thought Ring, younger than

he looks. He had expected the uncle of Jeanne Bonchamps to be an older man. De Feriet was frowning, staring into the fire.

'Yes,' he said reflectively. 'The cause was lost long ago. The Bonapartists war with England while true Frenchmen hide like rabbits in their burrows. The cause of Yves de Feriet is – Yves de Feriet – but *sainte vierge!*' he said suddenly. 'This is nothing to the point and I forget my manners. Captain Ring, I am grateful for this visit.'

'Which, I fear, cannot be a long one,' Ring put in.

'*C'est compris.* Jeanne has told me how you are situated. You should have dined with us, but it must be a glass of wine instead. She is bringing wine now – and taking long enough about it, *pardieu!*'

'Mademoiselle Bonchamps is a good sailor, it appears,' said Ring.

'We are all sailors here on Houat, captain. Jeanne loves the sea, and I – well, I have a little fleet down there in our harbour, as doubtless you've seen from your schooner. General de Feriet should be called Admiral de Feriet, *pardieu!*' He slapped his knee and gave his roaring laugh. 'Or perhaps Commodore, as your navy would have it. You shall salute me with eleven guns when next you pass Houat, captain.'

He laughed again, till he had to wipe his eyes with a silk handkerchief. Probably the contents of that empty bottle had something to do with his merriment, Ring thought as he politely echoed the laughter.

'And you have men to man your fleet, monsieur?' he asked.

'A dozen with their wives and children live on Houat.' De Feriet waved a big hand. '*En effet*, I am more like one of your English squires than an admiral. I employ them all, I look after them, they grow rich in my service –'

He broke off as an inner door opened to admit Jeanne carrying a tray with bottle and glasses, a different Jeanne from the sturdy fisher-girl who had accosted Ring on the twilight beach. Brown was her colour, high-waisted dress of russet velvet, brown hair close-braided on her head, round suntanned face demurely grave; but the monochrome was relieved by a collar of starched lace and an apron lavishly embroidered with gold thread in the Breton fashion. No one, Ring told himself as he rose to make his bow, would call

Mademoiselle Bonchamps a beauty but undeniably she made a charming picture.

'Well, well – no need for introductions, I believe,' De Feriet said as his niece, setting the tray on a table, dropped in a formal curtsey. '*Ma mie*, you have been a long time. Captain Ring is dying of thirst.'

'You asked for the Chinon, Yves,' she said, with a faint smile at Ring. 'It was at the back of the cellar, behind the cases of Saumur.'

De Feriet was already splashing red wine into two of the three glasses. He gave one to Jeanne and raised his own.

'Before we sit,' he said, 'you will permit us a little ceremony, captain. By destroying *Faucon* you have rendered us a service. We drink to that victory and to your further success.'

Ring, glancing from one to the other in some surprise as they drank, caught a gleam of amusement in the girl's brown eyes.

'I am naturally delighted to have been of service,' he said, 'but I don't quite see –'

'You shall wait a moment for my explanation but no longer for your wine.' The Baron handed him a brimming glass. 'First, however, indulge my curiosity by telling the story of your sea-fight. Jeanne, I know has heard it – I have the bones of it from her – but I would like to hear it from your own lips.' He set a chair for Jeanne between them and poured more wine for himself; she had taken only a sip of hers. 'As to the wine, captain, it is the '98 – a wine François Rabelais himself would have praised.'

Ring made his story short and omitted any mention of Verlay, as he had done when telling it to Jeanne. A secret agent, however detestable his trade, was not a subject for tittle-tattle on a French island. De Feriet alternately nodded approval and drank from his glass.

'I congratulate you, captain,' he said when Ring ended his tale. 'It was a bold action to challenge *Faucon*. I regret the damage to your ship but I understand it can be repaired. Any help I can give –'

'I have all I need, thank you. She will sail as soon as the morning tide lifts her.'

'Then you will leave me in your debt. You have relieved me

of a serious interference to my trade – *n'est-ce pas, ma mie?*'

Jeanne nodded. '*Faucon* nearly caught you in the lugger six weeks ago.'

'And in thus relieving me, captain,' De Feriet continued, 'you do your country a double service. Not only have you destroyed a *chasse-marée*, but you have also ensured that your admirals and squires continued to drink good claret.'

He ended with one of his tremendous laughs. Jeanne frowned at him.

'You should explain yourself to Captain Ring, Yves,' she told him.

'*D'accord* – though I suspect he has already guessed.' The Baron turned to Ring. 'Yes, captain, I am a *contrebandier*, a 'smuggler' as you would say. It has been my trade for seven years.' He shrugged his massive shoulders. 'A tradesman, you say, a *bourgeois*? But what would you have? A man must live, and a man causeless and proscribed must live for himself – your glass is empty, captain.'

Ring held it out to be refilled. It was a splendid wine, full-bodied and potent; two glasses, he decided, must be his limit if he was to get back to *Nonpareil* without mishap.

'You smuggle wine to England, then?' he said.

'And other things from England to France. Boots, clothing, hardware, a thousand items. They fetch high prices in blockaded France.' There was a new light in De Feriet's eyes as he leaned forward to wag a finger at the Englishman. 'There's a fortune to be made, captain, and I'm making it! I have my lines through the Brittany ports, my agents in Nantes. Houat is only my headquarters.'

'So you take money from both sides,' Ring commented drily.

For an instant the Baron looked angry. Then he laughed shortly. 'Sides? Bah! I've finished with taking sides, my friend. Ask yourself if I would see England conquer France, or Bonaparte conquer the world. Listen. I've learned that war profits no man except him who is clever enough to make both sides pay.'

Jeanne's level brows had drawn together in a frown as he talked. Now she interposed sharply.

'You do yourself injustice, Yves. You know well that you are loyal to the monarchy.'

De Feriet darted a glance at her and grinned a trifle sheepishly. '*Naturellement, ma mie.* Here's to the next Louis, eighteenth of the name!' He drained his glass. 'He won't find me backward when I'm needed. Meanwhile –'

He reached for the bottle and filled his glass; then, with a muttered apology, offered to fill Ring's. Ring declined politely, adding that in a few minutes he would be returning to his ship in the dark.

'You English are so prudent!' De Feriet said, with more than the hint of a sneer; undoubtedly the wine had gone to his head. '*Sainte vierge*, man, the path's easy enough to follow!'

'And of course your sentries would pick me up if I fell,' Ring countered equably.

'They let themselves be seen? Ah well –' The Baron shrugged – 'the fellows are fishermen, not Chouans. But you will understand, captain, that I have to take many precautions. Without them my continued residence on Houat would be precarious indeed.'

'I should think it must be precarious in any case so close to Bonaparte's mainland,' Ring ventured.

'Let us say delicately balanced. Persons of high authority in Nantes need my contraband supplies. In return for them they see that I am not harassed here.'

'Yet a *chasse-marée* harassed your lugger.'

'Ah – but *Faucon* was out of Finistère, where I have no such agreement. Except in the Vendée the Baron de Feriet is a proscribed man. Yet even in Nantes he must never be seen and recognised, even on Houat island he must tread warily.' De Feriet seemed to be somewhat sobered by his own words. 'If it were known in Nantes,' he went on, fixing a gloomy eye on Ring, 'that I entertain an English naval officer here, they would send the *gens d'armes* to arrest me. On the other hand, for the news that an English warship was lying disabled on Houat I could have won immunity from any further surveillance. And I'd have made them pay me for it too, *pardieu*!'

'But you would never have sent that news,' Jeanne said quickly.

'I? *Jamais de la vie.*' De Feriet took a long draught of wine. 'But there it is. My position, captain, is delicate, as you see. I must ask you to take yourself and your ship well clear of this island at the earliest opportunity. Mine is an extensive enterprise, built up over the years with much toil and some hazard. I have a score of agents in the wine-country of Vendée and Jeanne could tell you of a dozen others in her own land north of the Loire, among the Chouans. But if it is publicly brought to the notice of the Préfect in Nantes that I shelter enemy warships here he will be forced to take action. And then my business will be finished – *caput*.'

Jeanne shook her head at him, half-seriously. 'You talk more like a tradesman every day, Yves,' she said.

'*Tu as raison, ma mie.* It's time to talk of other things.'

'It's time for me to go,' said Ring, getting up.

'What – with wine still in the bottle?'

Ring laughed. 'Alas – yes, monsieur. I'm committed to return on board in half-an-hour's time. If I do not, my lieutenant and six men will come to look for me.'

De Feriet gave one of his noisy guffaws. 'Did I not say the English were prudent? But if that's the case, captain, you must certainly go. I don't want to find myself in a state of siege.'

'It won't be my fault, M. le Baron, if *Nonpareil* isn't out of Quiberon Bay before anyone sees her near your island.'

Jeanne had brought Ring's hat and boat-cloak and he added his formal thanks for their hospitality while he settled the cloak round his shoulders. The Baron shook his hand and seemed to hesitate before he spoke.

'*Écoutez.* If you have need to come here again, captain, be sure to come by night. Heave-to well clear of the island and send a boat to the jetty. I have a man always on watch there. To his challenge, reply "*Vive le roi*" – he will bring you to me.'

Ring thanked him somewhat perfunctorily. He thought it highly unlikely that he would visit Houat island again. He bowed over Jeanne's hand, made his final adieux, and went out into the cool night air. Pausing after a few paces to accustom his eyes to the darkness, he looked back and saw the two figures silhouetted against the orange glow of the open doorway, De Feriet with an arm round his niece's waist. The door closed and he began the walk back to his ship.

3

In the dark hour before dawn the flood-tide came creeping up
the sand, pushing its white loops of surf slowly forward until
they lapped the keel of the beached schooner. Lanterns flashed
yellow beams along her tilted deck and by their light slings and
planks were rigged outboard to form a bosun's chair, while
three dark figures came splashing back from laying-out a
kedge anchor and climbed aboard. With the first pale glimmer
of day Norie and his helpers were at work on the fitting of the
copper tingle. *Nonpareil*'s captain was keeping his word to the
Baron de Feriet; and – as always when a course of action was
resolved upon – he was using every effort to carry it out to the
best effect.

The wind had backed sou'-westerly a point and a thin flight
of rain drove through the lightening darkness. The change of
direction was if anything a help to *Nonpareil*'s departure, but
though the Houat beach was still sheltered from the rising
breeze the repair to her damaged side would get a thorough
testing when she came out from the lee of the island into the
Bay. Norie's work was at best a temporary job, but unless it
had to stand up to a real Biscay gale it should last until Captain
Cockburn could spare his auxiliary for a trip to Plymouth
dockyard.

Grey light grew to the ceaseless racket of the hammers. The
surf ran far beyond *Nonpareil*, dark waves surged under her
quarter, and she shifted uneasily like a sleeper unwillingly
waking. Her masts rocked, swung upright; the anchor, which
Ring had shifted to lie out astern, felt the first pull of the cable.
Before the yellow glimmer of the lanterns had paled under the
dawn light she was afloat and heaving on the stern cable. Her
keel lifted and touched, lifted and touched again as the
dripping cable began to come aboard, and then she was free
and slipping seaward over the incoming waves. Like a ghost a
sail writhed upwards from her foredeck, to flap and tauten
precisely as the anchor was broken out, and slowly she turned
her bows towards the waters of Quiberon Bay. Up went fore

and mainsails, foretopsail and staysail and gaff topsail, until she was stretching out like a greyhound on her course to clear the chain of rocks west of Houat – north by west for a league and then due west to run through the Teignouse Passage.

Ring sent a lookout to the masthead and turned an inquiring face to Breckinridge and Lunt as they came on deck.

'She's making some water, sir,' Breckinridge said, 'but it's little boy's piss now. A spell at the pumps every watch ought to keep her dry – unless we strike bad weather.'

'An' bad weather there could be, sir,' Lunt put in. 'Though I'd say by the wind veerin' that quick it'll be soon come, soon go.'

'Let's hope you're right, Mr Lunt,' Ring said. 'We'll hold on under all sail as long as we can. Hands to breakfast, if you please – and you too, Mr Breckinridge. Then you'll please to take the forenoon watch.'

'Aye aye, sir.' Breckinridge hesitated a moment. 'I think I should report, sir, that Turfrey brought a rabbit on board last night.'

'Indeed? Alive or dead?'

'Oh, dead, sir – snared it with a bit of cord while he was ashore on sentry duty, it seems. I dunno if you think snaring rabbits while on duty is a case for punishment, sir. Turfrey says he can stew it for your dinner.'

Ring grinned. 'I'll see how the stew turns out before pronouncing judgement.'

When Breckinridge had gone below he spent some moments trying to remember when he had last tasted rabbit stew. Home on leave as a midshipman – it must be all of a dozen years. Then he went for'ard to lean far out over the starboard rail; but with the wind over her quarter *Nonpareil* was showing very little of her new copper. He could trust Norie to have made a good job of it, though. Walking aft again, his glance fell on Houat island, already a mere dark streak under a sky flecked with grey clouds faintly tinged with rose, and for the first time that morning he recalled the previous evening's visit. An odd encounter, that. The Baron a queer customer, his niece – who called her uncle by his Christian name – pretty enough in a dumpy countrified way –

'There's hot coffee in the cabin, sir,' said Breckinridge, ducking out from the companionway. 'I'll take the deck, by your leave.'

Coffee! Ring could smell it. He went below to get it without another thought of Jeanne Bonchamps.

III

Captain Cockburn's Duty

1

The gale that had blown for thirty-six hours had blown itself out overnight and left a glittering morning. The sky was clearing to a pearly blue as the sun rose above the bank of cloud that was retreating eastward, and beneath it the dark-blue rollers flashed as their moving surfaces caught the light. *Nonpareil*, under plain sail, rode the smooth humped seas like a gull; and Robert Ring, pacing up and down the twenty feet of planking that substituted for a quarterdeck, was smiling his pleasure at the beauty of sea and sky and ship when he was suddenly aware of an answering smile, or rather a gap-toothed grin. The duty watch, six men on their hands and knees, were holystoning the deck abaft the mainmast, and the man nearest him was Abel Turfrey. Turfrey it was who had responded to what he no doubt took to be a friendly greeting from his captain.

Ring hastily contorted his features in a scowl and swung on his heel to pace aft, inwardly reprimanding himself. He was getting careless; a sea-officer in the Navy should keep his feelings under hatches. This lapse, he thought, was probably the consequence of yesterday's anxieties.

Nonpareil had reached her rendezvous ten miles southwest of the Pointe de Penmarch two days ago, in half-a-gale. Wind and sea had continued to rise, and while she was beating up and down, waiting for *Implacable*, Ring had never been free from a gnawing doubt as to whether Norie's repairs would stand up to the battering. But the tingle had held, and the inboard battening had proved staunch. The pump had been rigged and in use intermittently but was now dismantled, Lunt having pronounced her dry, and she was prettying-up ready to present herself before the senior officer of the diminutive squadron.

For *Implacable* had been sighted. Each time he turned in his pacing Ring's glance went to the speck of snowy white that every minute grew larger on the northern horizon. She would soon be hull-up; he would be submitting his report to Captain Cockburn before noon, possibly receiving an invitation to dine on board the 74. That his report concerning the fight with the *chasse-marée* would involve a tacit admission that he had exceeded his duty did not worry Ring. George Cockburn, a good sea-officer but otherwise (in Ring's opinion) not greatly endowed with brains, had this at least in common with his subordinate, that he threw himself heart and soul into any project he was engaged upon. He had been a midshipman under Nelson and never forgot it.

'Bear away a point,' Ring said to the helmsman, and the schooner headed to intercept *Implacable*'s course.

The triple towers of canvas grew against the sky, the high brown side with its double row of gunports loomed larger across the waves. When she was no more than a mile away her upper sails fluttered and vanished and at the same time a string of coloured bunting soared up to her yardarm. Ring had his telescope to his eye, but he could have guessed the signal correctly.

'Away longboat's crew, Mr Breckinridge, and see that it's smartly done.'

The boat splashed into the water while the schooner, brought to the wind, was still losing way. Ring stepped down into her and was rowed towards the 74, now hove-to at two cables distance. As always, he felt slightly overawed as the huge oaken wall of her side towered above him – she was so much vaster and more populous than his own little ship; six hundred men as opposed to his twenty. A Hampshire village yokel, he thought, must feel much the same when he approached London. But the feeling vanished as he stepped over the rail and saluted the quarterdeck, for he was no stranger here and Ward, first lieutenant, was an old friend. Captain Cockburn, a man of means, had all his crew clad in uniform blue and white, and what with the gold braid of the officers and the scarlet of the marine sentry abaft the helm the after-deck was a blaze of colour. The sober civilian rig of the two gentlemen with whom the captain was talking, one tall and stout and the other small and slim, looked out of place. The first lieutenant came towards him, his cheerful brown face split in a grin. Ward and Ring had been midshipmen together in *Montagu* in the days when that elderly 74 was chiefly employed in waylaying and searching merchantmen, and they had then evolved a somewhat puerile catch-phrase or watchword which Ward always insisted on using when they met.

'Whither bound, mister?' he said now as they touched fingers to hats.

'Homeward bound with a cargo of damn-all,' Ring responded according to rule.

There was no time for more, for Captain Cockburn had crossed the deck to them.

'Come aboard to report, sir,' Ring said, touching his hat again.

'Very well, Mr Ring. In my cabin, if you please.'

The marine sentry sprang to attention as Ring followed his senior through the glass-panelled door below the quarterdeck. Cockburn led on through the spacious main cabin into his day-cabin, a room four times the size of Ring's quarters aboard *Nonpareil*, and sitting down at the table waved the lieutenant to a chair opposite him. He took the carefully-written report Ring handed him and laid it aside.

'Your verbal report first,' he said shortly.

He was a big man, with a large mottled face whose round pale-blue eyes gave him the look of a slightly apoplectic infant. He heard Ring's concise account of his doings with a somewhat abstracted air, though he interjected terse commendations of the schooner's action with the *chasse-marée* and a question or two concerning the smuggler-baron and his niece.

'Report approved, Mr Ring,' he said with a nod and a smile when it was finished. 'Very commendable, very commendable indeed. I shan't fail to mention it in my next dispatch to their lordships. As to that feller Verney, Verlay, whatever his name was, you acted correctly, quite correctly. Damn me, if a spy likes to pretend he's a Frenchman he must take his chance with the rest of the Frogs. But *Nonpareil*, now – that shot-hole's soundly repaired?'

'It bore a moderate gale, sir, but I wouldn't guarantee it against another. She needs dry-docking, in fact.'

The captain frowned. 'Then she must have it. But I've a task for her before you can take her to Plymouth, a task which – well, you'd better hear about it now.'

Cockburn took a folded paper from the drawer under the table-top and hesitated, biting his lip. Then he unfolded the paper with sudden decision and stared hard at his lieutenant.

'Mr Ring,' he said solemnly, 'I'm going to confide in you. I do so because you – um – have some knowledge of France and the – um – lingo, which is more than I have, or my officers either. And I believe you've been in France.'

He was, Ring perceived, being tactful; few post-captains would have bothered.

'My mother was French, sir, of course,' he said to help him out, 'but it's a long time since I visited France myself.'

'Never mind, never mind. I believe you can assist me. This –' Cockburn tapped the paper with his forefinger – 'is from the Marquess Wellesley at the Foreign Office and it's marked 'Secret'. Listen to what he says. "His Majesty having determined to make an effort to rescue the person of King Ferdinand the Seventh from the hands of the French, and to restore that monarch to his subjects, I have received His Majesty's commands to direct you to proceed with the ships which have been placed under your orders by the Lords Commissioners of the Admiralty to the immediate execution of this important service." ' He lowered the paper to stare at his subordinate. 'You know anything of this King Ferdinand?'

Ring concealed his rising excitement. 'Yes, sir – he's the king of Spain by rights, but Bonaparte forced him to abdicate and put his own brother Joseph on the throne instead of him. Ferdinand's been a prisoner in France for the past three years.'

'Very well. Now, then –' the captain resumed his reading. ' "After having received on board the agents who are to be employed on this occasion, you will proceed to Quiberon Bay or to such other point upon the coast of France as you may judge most advisable for landing these persons. You will concert with them the means of embarking them either in the event of the success or of the failure of the plan. In the event of the safe arrival of the King of Spain on board your ship, you

will act according to the directions contained in my –" '
Cockburn broke off and slapped the paper down on the table.
'But never mind that. You've heard all the orders I've got. Give
me your opinion of the plan.'

'First-rate, sir,' Ring said at once. 'A smashing blow at
Bonaparte's prestige and a vast encouragement to our allies in
the Peninsula. If,' he added, 'it can be brought off.'

'Ha!' Cockburn jabbed a finger at him. 'That's the whole of
the trouble.' He leaned across the table and lowered his voice.
'Not a word of this goes beyond this cabin. You understand?'

'I understand, sir.'

'Very well, then. I've embarked these two agents at
Plymouth – you saw 'em as you came aboard, doubtless.
Spanish nobles, both of 'em. The big feller's the Baron de Kolli
and the other's Don Felicito Maura. I've concerted with 'em, as
Wellesley calls it, and my further orders are simply to land 'em
and then stand by to pick 'em up again. When I've done that
I've done my whole duty.'

He paused and looked at Ring as if awaiting his comment.
Ring declined the invitation; he was certainly not going to
express opinions about a post-captain's duty.

'Yes, sir,' he said without inflection. 'And the landing, I take
it, will be made from *Nonpareil*.'

'Yes, yes, of course,' the captain said testily. 'But that's not
my point.' He lowered his voice still farther. 'I'll be frank with
you, Ring. I don't think Kolli and Maura are up to this
mission. Plenty of zeal, plenty of courage, but lacking the
brains. You heard what this dispatch says. "His Majesty having
determined to make an effort," and "this important service".
Damn me, no important service I was ever on was as ill
prepared as this one! And as to King George's effort, I'm the
sole representative of that and a damned set of half-measures it
is – God bless His Majesty!' he added hurriedly.

'Perhaps, sir, you could tell me something of the plan,' Ring
suggested.

Cockburn eyed him uncertainly for a moment and then
nodded. 'I don't see why not. You'll have to take charge of the
landing in any case. Not a word to anyone else, mind.'

He interspersed his explanation with impatient comments,
but the few details were clear enough apart from the inception

of the plan, which appeared to have developed from haphazard contacts between the Spanish agents and exiled French royalists. The place and time of the landing on the French coast had been already fixed upon: the beach of La Turballe north of the Pointe du Croisic, on one of the three nights from 10th to 12th September. ('The dolts take tide and weather for granted, apparently.') The Spaniards were to go to a solitary hut above the beach, on the southern edge of the salt marsh, where a Chouan royalist would be waiting. Arrangements would then be made for their surreptitious journey to the Château de Valençay where King Ferdinand was confined. ('Though how they're to travel fifty leagues without being twigged I'm damned if I can see.') At Valençay they were to seek out a man named Gril Picart, head stableman at the Château but secretly a loyal Chouan, and with him devise the means of getting the King away. Their route back to the coast with their royal charge would depend on circumstances but they were to head for Erdeven, some 18 miles up the coast from their landing-place, arriving there by the last day of September. Here *Implacable* would be waiting to take them off, cruising offshore south of the Ile de Groix; if they had not arrived by 7th October she was to assume the attempt had failed and return to Plymouth to report. The Spaniards had not considered how they would apprise the 74 of their return ('Thought they'd stand on the beach and shout, I suppose') but had agreed with Cockburn that they would light a fire on the Pointe d'Erdeven precisely at midnight as a signal.

'So you see how it is, Ring,' Cockburn finished, a frown on his heavy features. '*Implacable* plays no active part in this expedition. She's no more than a floating base. I set these Don Escapados ashore, pick 'em up again – with or without Ferdinand of Spain – and my duty's done. It's not enough, and that's my opinion. What's yours? I ask it,' he added earnestly, 'as one servant of His Majesty to another.'

Ring considered for a moment. The idea of rescuing the King of Spain from the clutches of Bonaparte had taken strong hold on his imagination, and though the ramshackle plan appeared impossibly risky he didn't want to condemn it on that account.

'The landing and the taking-off should give us no

problems,' he said slowly, 'given a calm night with a minimum of surf. There's no French post nearer La Turballe than the battery on the Croisic, and Erdeven point is a sandy spit with nothing inland of it but marshland. But I take it your anxieties, sir, are concerned with other matters.'

'Aye, by God!' The captain sound impatient. 'The Dons, for a start. They've to pass as Frenchmen among Frenchmen for a fortnight at least and I don't see them doing it. If De Kolli's French isn't better than his English they'll smoke him as soon as he opens his mouth. You'll be able to judge for yourself when you meet them at dinner – you'll dine with me, of course.' He glanced at the clock on the bulkhead. 'In half-an-hour's time.'

'Thank you, sir.'

'But my anxieties, as you called them – and you were damned right, Ring – are chiefly about what happens to 'em on this damned chancy journey to and from the Château at Valençay. D'you know the place?'

'I know it's thirty miles south of the Loire, sir, because I read the *Moniteur* whenever I can get hold of it and the Château was mentioned in it some while ago. Bonaparte presented it to his minister Talleyrand. It's all of fifty leagues from the sea, as you said.'

Cockburn nodded grimly. 'Fifty leagues of enemy territory. We push these two Spaniards into it and that's all the help we give. I don't feel I'm doing my full duty.'

'I don't see that you can do anything more, sir,' Ring said. 'If you were thinking of a landing-party –'

'Out of the question, of course. This is one of those damned underhand operations for civilians only. But I tell you, Ring, I'd be happier if I knew these – these Spanish lambs were in the charge of a competent shepherd. They're going into a den of wolves.'

'Not quite that, sir. In Brittany and Vendée they'll find more than a few folk ready to take the risk of helping them. If you recall my report, you'll remember that the Baron de Feriet told me of his many agents north and south of the Loire, Chouans and others who help him with his –'

'By *God*!'

Captain Cockburn's fist banged down on the table and his

blue eyes, round as saucers, stared at Ring as if his lieutenant was a benevolent apparition.

'The very man – under my nose, damn me!' He gobbled slightly in his excitement. 'Think he'd do it, Ring – take charge for a start, set the Spaniards on their way?'

'I believe he would, sir,' said Ring with some reluctance. 'The Baron claims to be a royalist and he's fought for the royalist cause against Bonaparte. But – by your leave, sir – this is a secret mission and there's nothing in your orders –'

'I'm considering my duty, Mr Ring!' the captain snapped; his frown was transient and he at once regained his rapt enthusiasm. 'This Baron How-d'ye-call-him can help us as no one else can. There'll be no need to tell him our objective. The two Spanish agents are to be got across country to – what's the nearest town to Valençay?'

'Blois, sir.'

'To Blois, then. We can tell your man they're part of a British scheme to thwart a secret plan of Bonaparte's. That's it!' Cockburn thumped the table again. 'Now, then. How can I meet this smuggler feller?'

Ring explained De Feriet's instructions in the event of his returning to Houat. 'There are the Spaniards to consider, sir,' he added. 'Will they approve this plan?'

'They'll jump at it. They pretend confidence, but they're both nervous about stepping into French territory on the strength of arrangements made God knows how long ago. So would I be.' The captain thought for a moment. 'Today's the ninth – by God, we've no time to waste! How's the tide in Quiberon Bay?'

'Slack water of the flood at half-past eight, sir.'

'*Nonpareil* can make in at sunset and return at daybreak. I'll take De Kolli with me to Houat tonight.' Cockburn stood up and Ring did the same. 'Dinner in fifteen minutes, Mr Ring. We shall come aboard *Nonpareil* this afternoon.'

'Aye aye, sir,' said Ring.

2

Dinner with *Implacable*'s captain was a very different affair from the meals Ring was accustomed to on board his schooner, lukewarm snacks rushed aft from the galley by one of the ship's boys, cooked with enough salt to preclude the emergence of any other flavour. The 74 was only three days out of port and Captain Cockburn hadn't wasted his time in the Plymouth victualling yard. Abel Turfrey's rabbit stew, tasty though it had been, hadn't the sheer excellence of the saddle of mutton that followed the soup, and the fresh baker's bread was more than welcome after weeks of purser's hard-tack. It was satisfactory, too, to know that while he was thus enjoying himself *Nonpareil's* longboat was busy ferrying some of these luxuries to replenish the schooner's food store.

The table in the big cabin was spread with a white linen cloth, stewards in clean white jackets pattered in and out with the dishes; the noon sunlight flooding in through the row of slanting stern-windows sent barred patterns sliding to and fro across the deck as the 74, hove-to, rolled slowly on the long Atlantic swell. The motion was plainly causing the Baron de Kolli some discomfort but he controlled it manfully and produced a wan smile in response to Ring's raised glass and polite '*Salud!*'

Formal introductions had taken place on the quarterdeck before dinner, Ring being presented as the commanding officer of *Nonpareil*; there was no mention then or during dinner of the Spaniards' mission or the part he was to play in it. De Kolli, a large man with an autocratic manner and the smouldering eye of a zealot, spoke English fairly well apart from some difficulty with his sibilants, but his companion was less fluent. Don Felicito Maura was slight of figure and dark-skinned, and his thin mobile face and keen glance displayed a quicker apprehension than De Kolli's. Ring found him more likeable than the elder Spaniard and more conversable when French was being spoken. Cockburn had invited his first lieutenant to make a fifth at the table and Ring would have liked to exchange news and reminiscence with Ward, but the captain's hint that he should assess the quality of his guests' command of the French tongue constituted an order and he obeyed it. A general and slightly laboured conversation in English – the making of a *tortilla*, Plymouth, the adverse winds on the voyage out – occupied the first courses and then Cockburn somewhat pointedly engaged

Ward in talk about the trimming of *Implacable*'s holds and Ring took his chance. His own French had lost what little rustiness it had acquired when he was talking with De Feriet on Houat. His questions to the two Spaniards concerning the progress of the war in Spain were answered briefly by De Kolli and more eagerly by Maura, and his ear could detect no serious flaws in their pronunciation, though their French (unlike his own which had a Breton accent) was Parisian in tone. Much would depend, he thought, on what rôle or disguise they were required to adopt for their hazardous journey into France.

The stewards removed the last dishes, leaving the decanter. Cockburn nodded at his first lieutenant, and Ward, excusing himself on the ground of work to be done on deck, left the cabin. The captain filled his glass and passed the decanter to Maura on his left.

'First, gentlemen,' he said, 'I'll tell you what you've already guessed – that Mr Ring here will be responsible for landing you on the coast.'

'Tomorrow night,' nodded De Kolli.

'Tomorrow or the next night. It will depend on weather and sea. We have a dangerous coast here, a lee shore, and Quiberon Bay is no place for a seventy-four. You'll be prepared, therefore, to embark in *Nonpareil*.'

'Mr Ring has been told of the rendezvous?' Maura inquired. 'He agrees that the place is a suitable one for landing?'

'Of course, of course,' Cockburn said with a transient frown. 'And he knows these coasts very well, señor. But I have further news for you, and good news. We've located a man, a royalist Frenchman, who can greatly aid your expedition if we can enlist his help.'

He told of Ring's landing on Houat and visit to Port Halai. 'This Baron de Feriet,' he added, 'appears to have a ready-made network of helpers in the district you've to travel through – a perfect godsend for your purpose.'

'Zis is not necessary,' De Kolli objected. 'Our arrangements are made for us already.'

'You can only assume so, Baron,' Cockburn said impatiently. 'You told me yourself you know nothing of what's to be done after you're met at La Turballe.'

'At Valençay we meet anuzzer man,' De Kolli retorted.

'There's fifty leagues to be covered before you do. As I understand it, these plans of yours were laid some weeks ago – God knows what might have happened by now. We need to use every means to ensure your success, don't we?'

'This is true,' Maura said eagerly. 'Monsieur de Feriet has fight for King Louis,' he went on, choosing his words with difficulty. 'So, then, he will be happy to give help to His Majesty of Spain.'

De Kolli fingered his square chin, scowling. 'I like it not,' he growled. 'The expedition is udmost zegret. To tell to this Frenchman, a stranger –'

'And there you're damned right, Baron,' Cockburn broke in. 'De Feriet mustn't know your real objective. We tell him you want to travel to Blois on a secret mission for the British Government and ask him to help – that's all. If he won't, or can't, no harm's done. But if you let this opportunity pass you may well regret it. Mr Ring will tell you the same.'

'Of course, sir. The more help the señores can get in France the better.'

Ring answered confidently because it was expected to him, but inwardly he was doubtful. There had been much of the braggart about De Feriet; his immunity in Nantes and his army of agents might not be so effective as he had boasted. Don Felicito was speaking in rapid Spanish to his senior, who still looked undecided.

'*Muy bien,*' De Kolli said at last; and to Cockburn, 'What then do you propose?'

'That we see the Baron de Feriet without delay,' Cockburn said firmly. 'It's forty sea-miles to Houat island, wind's fair, sea moderating, and *Nonpareil* can put us ashore there in –' he looked a question at Ring.

'Six hours if this wind holds, sir.'

'And we're directed to land after nightfall. We should sail at four bells, then.' The captain glanced from Maura to De Kolli. 'I suggest that I myself, with Mr Ring and one of you two gentlemen, should land on Houat.'

'I will go,' De Kolli said.

'Good. Be ready, Baron, to transfer to the schooner within the hour. – The decanter stands with you, Don Felicito. We've time at least for a toast, gentlemen, and it's to a successful mission and a happy return.'

Ten minutes later Ring was in the longboat on his way back to *Nonpareil*, Cockburn having ordained that the 74's gig should bring him and De Kolli over in half-an-hour's time. His head was full of what he had heard on board *Implacable*. The daring of the plan, its dangerous inadequacy even, appealed strongly to that side of Robert Ring which loved a gamble provided the stakes were high enough; and here the stake was the throne of Spain. It was a pity, he felt, that he couldn't take a more active part in it.

3

The half-moon hung in a night sky almost clear of cloud, but the haze drifting into Quiberon Bay from the Atlantic diffused its light. Houat island was an indeterminate blackness growing out of a faintly-luminous mist as the schooner's cockboat ploughed its steady way towards Port Halai. The boat had put off from *Nonpareil* at the beginning of the first watch, leaving the schooner at anchor in eight fathoms a mile off the beach where she had careened three nights ago. The occupants of the boat had spoken little during twenty minutes of pulling, for the presence of Abel Turfrey at the sculls forbade discussion of the matter uppermost in their minds. Now Captain Cockburn spoke from the sternsheets where he sat beside the Baron de Kolli.

'Lights right ahead, Mr Ring.'

'That'll be the houses of Port Halai, sir,' Ring said from his place in the bows. 'The jetty's directly below them.'

'Ah,' said Cockburn, and lapsed into silence.

Nonpareil carried only two boats, longboat and cockboat, and in view of the settled weather and calm sea it had been decided to use the latter. When it came to employment on anything concerned with a secret mission, Cockburn had observed, the fewer hands the better; and a single oarsman could pull the cockboat with three passengers. Ring had chosen Turfrey for this duty, partly because it was to be a long pull and Turfrey was undoubtedly the strongest man of his crew but also because the man semed to have more intelligence and discretion than the average lower-deck hand. The ex-poacher had picked up the knack of oarsmanship as quickly as he had grasped the other details of practical seamanship and his tireless strokes had brought them smoothly to their destination.

'Voices and movement yonder,' Cockburn said suddenly. 'And moving lights at sea-level.'

Ring twisted round on the bow thwart to look ahead. The two or three lights of the houses were close above now, and the flicker of lanterns lower down gave a momentary glimpse of the outline of the little stone jetty half-a-cable away. The sound of men's voices and the rattle of cordage came more loudly on the faint but steady breeze.

'All will be well, yes?' De Kolli sounded more than a little uneasy.

'Preparing for a night fishing trip, probably,' Ring said reassuringly.

They neared the low stone wall of the jetty with the narrow harbour entrance opening on its right. When the cockboat was a pistol-shot from it a voice challenged sharply in French. Ring stood up in the bows.

'Easy,' he told Turfrey; and shouted De Feriet's password. '*Vive le roi!*'

'What do you want?' demanded the voice.

'To speak with Monsieur de Feriet.'

'Ah? And who are you?'

'You can tell him *Nonpareil* is here.'

There was a pause and the sound of flint and steel. A lit lantern appeared above the low wall of the jetty, towards which the boat's way had carried her, and the half-seen figure behind the lantern spoke again, warningly.

'I've a loaded musket here, *mes amis*. Enter the harbour, bring your boat alongside the lugger and stay there. *Et pas de tricherie, comprenez?*'

Ring translated these instructions for the captain's benefit and told Turfrey to give way. The boat crept past the end of the jetty into the tiny basin, where the shapes of four or five fishing-vessels lay on their starboard hand and a larger vessel, two-masted and showing a light from a port on her quarter, lay alongside the short quay on the opposite side. As the cockboat sheered up below the lugger's rail the man with the lantern arrived to inspect them from above.

'You have timed your visit to the minute, messieurs,' he said more civilly. 'The General is on his way down even now. You can come aboard.'

Cockburn needed no translation of this and swung his heavy body up and over the rail. Ring helped De Kolli to follow, and with a word to Turfrey climbed onto the lugger's deck. The lantern and the hazy moonlight showed him her yards laid ready with the sails bent for hoisting. Two men who had been coiling ropes straightened themselves to stare at the new arrivals, and the lantern-bearer had begun a blasphemous exhortation to get on with their work when he broke off suddenly and stepped to the quayside rail with his lantern held high. The Baron de Feriet sprang down to the deck and turned to give his hand to a smaller figure in a hooded cloak. The lantern-light gleamed on braided brown hair as Jeanne Bonchamps threw back her hood, and Ring caught her quick smile as she saw and recognised him. De Feriet had seen the strangers on his deck in the same instant.

'*Sainte vierge!*' he said sharply. 'Whom have we here?'

Ring stepped forward. 'Robert Ring of *Nonpareil*, Monsieur le Baron. I have with me two gentlemen who desire to ask your help.'

'*Vraiment?* Do you not, Monsieur Ring, presume too far upon a very short acquaintance?'

This was not welcoming. Ring hastened to improve matters.

'I hope not,' he said quickly. 'This is an affair of great import in the fight against Bonaparte.'

'It is urgent?'

'Most urgent. And confidential,' Ring added, with a glance at the lantern-bearer who was listening with interest.

'Then down to my cabin.'

De Feriet led the way down the short ladder, with Captain Cockburn (who was showing some annoyance at being made to play second fiddle) close behind him and De Kolli descending third. Ring stood aside to give precedence to the girl, who replied to his bow with a slight inclination of her head; the smile was gone now, and the quick glance she threw at him was a questioning one. The lugger's cabin was small and with little headroom but well-appointed, with a table occupying the after end and cushioned lockers along the bulkheads. A lamp shed yellow light from above the table. The frowning impatience with which De Feriet waved his visitors to seats at the table warned Ring that he must be quick if his senior officer was not to have an apoplexy, and he rattled through his introductions at a very unmannerly speed. He was relieved to see the instant change in the smuggler-baron's demeanour. De Feriet made two graceful bows, begged to present his niece Mademoiselle Bonchamps, and apologised for his curtness.

'For excuse,' he added, 'I must plead that I am on the point of setting out in this lugger for an absence that will endure for a week at least. The Baron de Kolli, I hope, will indulge my lack of respect at our first meeting.' He turned to Cockburn and spoke in English. 'And to you, my dee-ar fellow the captain, I give one damn big apology.'

Cockburn cleared his throat. '*Merci, monsieur. J'espère que –*'

Here his French failed him and he nodded impatiently at his lieutenant. Before Ring could speak, however, De Kolli, a frown on his heavy face, was addressing De Feriet.

'We are to discuss a most secret matter, monsieur, which must not go beyond the four of us round this table.'

As he spoke his glance went to Jeanne, who had seated herself on the locker against the for'ard bulkhead. De Feriet smiled and shook his head.

'What I hear, Monsieur le Baron, Mademoiselle Bonchamps must hear. She is not only my niece but a partner in my business also – and, as I guess, it is my business that has led to the honour of your visit. Shall we, then, proceed?'

De Kolli nodded, but doubtfully and without looking at Jeanne. Ring swiftly decided that it was unnecessary to translate this exchange for the captain and launched at once into his explanation of their plan and needs. De Feriet listened in silence, one hand stroking his moustache, his narrowed gaze scanning his three visitors.

'So, then,' he said when Ring had finished, 'we have two men landed at La Turballe tomorrow or the next night. They are to deal a powerful blow at Bonaparte's prestige. To do this they must travel in secret from the coast to Blois, some fifty leagues. The other can pass as a Frenchman?'

'His French is as good as mine, at least.'

'Then he can pass.' De Feriet turned to the Spaniard. 'You and your companion, as I understand it, Monsieur le Baron, have a rendezvous with some helpers – they will doubtless be Chouans – at La Turballe. Beyond that you know nothing of your promised aid?'

There was incredulity and a touch of scorn in his tone and De Kolli reddened and answered sharply.

'When we reach Valençay we shall –'

He stopped dead, obviously aware of his mistake. De Feriet, just as obviously, knew that a mistake had been made. There was a dawning comprehension in the gaze he now transferred to Ring, but Ring was already covering-up as best he could.

'Monsieur de Kolli meant Blois – at Blois, perhaps, he and Don Felicito may find further help. But you perceive, monsieur,' he went on quickly, 'where your help, if you would give it, would be of very great value. You have agents, you told me, scattered across the region through which these gentlemen must pass in secret, anti-Bonapartists true to the royalist cause. If their help could be relied upon instead of arrangements made weeks ago and by now, possibly, no longer –'

'Yes, yes – I understand.' De Feriet reflected for a moment. 'I believe it may be done. But I think, Monsieur Ring, I could give more assistance if I knew the object of this mission.'

De Kolli leaned forward. He had recovered his self-possession and spoke with portentous emphasis.

'That is out of the question, monsieur. Too much has been said already. I am bound in honour to the British Foreign Secretary to say no more.'

Ring noted the flicker of De Feriet's eyes at the mention of De Kolli's sponsor; at least, he thought, the Spaniard's imprudence had made plain the peculiar importance of his mission. De Feriet must be aware of the royal prisoner at Valençay and could hardly fail to guess what was intended. But the smuggler merely shrugged and nodded.

'*Entendu*. I shall do what I can. There is little time and it will mean much work for me.' He paused, stared at Captain Cockburn, and spoke abruptly in English. 'And who will pay me for this goddam work – Spain or England?'

There was a shocked silence while the captain, taken aback,

returned the stare blankly.

'Monsieur,' he said slowly after a moment, 'I'm not empowered to offer – it wasn't expected that –'

De Feriet's huge guffaw cut him short and he found himself clapped jocularly on the shoulder.

'It is my damn good joke, captain – never mind, my dee-ar fellow.' The Frenchman, suddenly serious again, addressed De Kolli. 'How long have you allowed for your journey – to Blois, Monsieur le Baron?'

Ring's glance went past De Kolli to Jeanne, who hadn't spoken since she entered the cabin. She was sitting composedly with downcast eyes, hands folded in the lap of her russet gown; but she looked up quickly to meet his gaze and he saw then the anxiety in her brown eyes. It was a fugitive glimpse, for Cockburn was muttering irritably in his ear.

'Confound the feller! Is he playing with us, Ring?'

'I think not, sir,' Ring muttered back. 'I fancy he's guessed what we're after and he's going to help.'

'*Ça va*,' De Feriet was saying. 'You may do it in a week, perhaps less.' He looked at Ring. 'And afterwards – I say nothing of the objective – your ship will pick up these gentlemen from the coast, presumably. Where? I ask,' he added, 'because there too I may be able to assist them.'

'From the Pointe d'Erdeven,' Ring said with a glance at the captain.

'Ha! And Erdeven is an easy day's march from the mill at Callac, where the miller is a good Chouan and a friend of mine. But that can wait. Let us consider this landing – Jeanne, *ma mie*, please to bring the chart.'

The girl rose, took a rolled chart from the rack on the bulkhead beside her, and spread it on the table, remaining to watch while the four men bent over it.

'The Rade de Croisic, three leagues across the water from us here.' De Feriet traced the shore-line with a forefinger. 'Batteries on the Croisic and at Castelli. A long beach between, deserted except for fishermen's hovels at La Turballe.' He looked up. 'Jeanne, you know this shore better than I do. Where is this hut Monsieur le Baron speaks of?'

'Here.' She leaned above them to point. 'There are low dunes and behind them a marsh where they have made salt-pans. The hut – it is of stone, and the only one – stands on the high grass dyke to the south of the marsh, a hundred paces perhaps beyond high-water mark. As to the huts at La Turballe, I have often landed on this beach and the last time, ten days ago, they were deserted and half ruined.'

She spoke rapidly and without hesitation, but Ring's ear detected an odd tonelessness in her voice; she was not enthusiastic about this plan, he thought. De Kolli was evidently much encouraged. His little eyes were gleaming as he addressed the Frenchman in confident tones.

'This is very well, monsieur. We shall reach this stone hut, thanks to Captain Cockburn, either tomorrow or the next night. Shall we then find one of your agents awaiting us there?'

De Feriet hesitated but only for a second. 'For many reasons that is impossible, Monsieur le Baron. We shall have to assume that your original plan remains in force, to that extent at least. You must understand that before I can arrange anything I must reach Nantes – whither indeed I was bound when you arrived.' He glanced up at Jeanne. 'My niece is here to bid me farewell. Had you come an hour later you would have found me gone.'

'A sign that fortune is with us,' De Kolli exclaimed.

'The omens are so far propitious,' agreed De Feriet, frowning. 'But the essential first step lies with you, monsieur.' He levelled a monitory finger. 'Who will meet you I do not know, but he will know of me if he is a Chouan. You will tell him that he is to bring you and your comrade to me in Nantes, at number ten Rue de la Boucherie. That is my headquarters and a safe house. Only from there can I set you on your way.'

'But –'

'There will be no danger. It is no more than five leagues from La Turballe to Nantes, and a Chouan can bring you there in a day by way of the Brière and the Loire bank. The house is close to Sainte-Croix church. When you reach it –'

Here Ring's attention was distracted by Captain Cockburn, who for some minutes had been fidgeting and growling and now demanded to be told what was going on. Ring told him in a few rapid sentences. Cockburn's satisfaction was apparent; but before he could voice it all proceedings in the cabin were halted by a piercing yell from the deck overhead, followed by a gabble of angry voices.

'*Sainte vierge!*' De Feriet got up and strode to the ladder. '*Qu'est-ce qu'arrive?*'

Ring hurried on deck after him. He had heard Turfrey's voice among the rest. The hazy moonlight revealed two dark figures hurling objurgations from the rail, a third man hopping about the deck in apparent pain, and a guttering lantern lying on its side. De Feriet righted the lantern with an oath and was immediately assailed by a triple torrent of angry explanations from his men. Stepping to the rail, Ring saw that the cockboat was prudently lying several fathoms away. He ordered it peremptorily to come alongside.

'What's all this, Turfrey?'

Turfrey's face was dimly visible as the boat came to rest below the rail. The wide grin on it vanished at the threatening note in Ring's voice.

'So please ye, sir –'

'*Taisez-vous!*' De Feriet bellowed, quelling the clamour of the French seamen. 'What has your man to say? I can get no sense from mine.'

The other three had come up from the cabin and were behind him as he stood at Ring's side. Turfrey, aware of an audience, stood up in the boat and delivered his story in his deep countryman's voice.

''Twas like this, sir. Seein' as how you was gone some time an' me bein' a bit anxious-like, I bobbed my head up to look along the deck an' there was this Frenchy, him with the lantern. What were he a-doin', sir, but lyin' flat with his ear agin the deck planks.'

'*Le scélérat!*' ejaculated De Feriet.

Encouraged, Turfrey (evidently a born story-teller, thought Ring exasperatedly) attempted to delay his dénouement.

'Aye, mounseer – a-listenin' to the gab in the cabin, that's what he were a-doin',' he pronounced impressively. 'Ah, thinks I, 'twon't do for the captain, that won't. Now mark ye, sir, what had this bugger done but set down his lantern behind him on the deck, him lyin' flat as I said, an' the lantern a span from his bum. Ho, thinks I –'

'Cut it short, man!' Ring snapped.

'Aye aye, sir.' Turfrey's measured utterance suddenly took wings. 'I ups with a scull, slides blade across deck, an' shoves the lantern agin the Frenchy's rump, sir.'

Before Ring could make any comment on this De Feriet, with a howl of rage, had seized the offending eavesdropper and was frog-marching him across the deck, to send him flying over the rail onto the quay with a final savage kick.

'Resourceful feller, that man of yours,' Captain Cockburn said in Ring's ear. 'How much d'you reckon the Frenchman heard?'

Ring leaned from the rail. 'How long was he listening, Turfrey?'

'Three or four minutes, sir, not more.'

'How do you know?'

'The lantern was movin' about for'ard afore then, sir.'

As they were speaking Jeanne's voice could be heard explaining to the anxious De Kolli what had happened, and now De Feriet broke in with cheerful reassurances.

'My dear Baron, no harm is done, my word upon it. Alphonse Barac is incurably inquisitive – I have punished him a dozen times – but the scoundrel is loyal as are all my men. M. Ring's seaman acted very properly,' he added. '*Sainte vierge!* Barac will not sit for a week!'

His roar of laughter served to soothe De Kolli's anxieties as well as to suggest that the arrangement of a secret journey to Blois held no problems for Yves de Feriet. A moment later he remarked more seriously that the hour was late and the ebb running; and Captain Cockburn, taking the hint, summoned his laborious French for leavetaking.

A hand touched Ring's arm and he found Jeanne beside him.

'Monsieur Ring,' she said hurriedly, 'the waters off La Turballe are shallow for a long way out. You will have to make in at high water and anchor far offshore.'

'My thanks, mademoiselle.' Ring was amused. 'But the Royal Navy has charts of your coast, you know.'

'Take care,' she said.

Her tone was so serious that Ring, about to step down into the boat, paused to glance at her face. It might have been a trick of the moonlight but he thought she looked frightened.

De Kolli was already in the sternsheets. Cockburn embarked last and the cockboat pushed off from the lugger's side. De Feriet's voice followed them.

'Rely upon me, *mes amis. Adieu!*'

The cockboat slid out through the narrow harbour entrance and settled on its course to return to the schooner. Five minutes later Ring, peering astern at the jetty fast fading into the misty night, saw the lugger steal out like a black ghost and stand towards the south-east.

'De Feriet's away for Nantes, sir,' he said. 'He doesn't waste his time.'

'No. And I don't think I've wasted mine.' The captain sounded a trifle unsure of it. 'At any rate,' he added more firmly, 'I've damned well done all I can – and that, Mr Ring, is a sea-officer's whole duty.'

'Yes, sir,' said Ring.

IV

The Landing

1

De Feriet had said that the omens were propitious and Robert Ring could agree with him. He had been long enough up and down the northern Biscay coast to know that the days when a boat could land on those deeply-indented rock-bound shores were few and far between; that the present spell of calm weather, brief though it was certain to be, should coincide with the plan to land at La Turballe seemed providential. On all the Quiberon coasts the surf and the perpetual onshore winds made landing hazardous, and though at La Turballe – as his chart showed him – there was a sandy beach four miles long with no reefs or shoals the Atlantic rollers could beat up as formidable a surf there as they did on the *côte sauvage* of the Quiberon peninsula itself. The secret planners who had stipulated three September nights as the only dates when a landing would be awaited must, he thought, have been ignorant of their own coasts and the problems of wind and tide. As it was, they had been lucky. One of the three nights had passed, for it had been 10th September when Captain Cockburn's conception of his duty had led to the fruitful visit to Houat. But the glass was steady, and Lunt the boatswain, who had more experience of Biscay weather than any other man aboard *Nonpareil*, declared that there would be no notable shift or strengthening of the wind for forty-eight hours at least.

Despite this hopeful circumstance and their good fortune in enlisting De Feriet's help – in the nick of time, too – Ring was uneasy, though he couldn't tell why. Perhaps the odd little incident of the eavesdropper on the lugger had unsettled his confidence. Perhaps it was the expression on Jeanne

Bonchamps' face, glimpsed as he stepped down into the cockboat: dread, even horror, he had thought to see there, as if she looked beyond him to some frightening possibility in the future. It could have been a trick of the moonlight, of course, but it lingered obstinately in his memory all the same. But different from this unease, which might be baseless, was his growing anxiety about the problems De Kolli and Maura would have to face after their landing – and after they had gone beyond whatever help De Feriet might afford.

Reflecting on these problems in the middle watch, while *Nonpareil*, hove-to two miles north of Houat, was waiting for daybreak, Ring was surprised at the depth of his own involvement with the rescue expedition. The more he perceived how heavily the dice were loaded against its success the more anxious he became that it should succeed. The idea of rescuing an imprisoned monarch from a castle in the heart of enemy territory was so implausible, so out-of-period in this humdrum nineteenth century, that he felt he was assisting at the re-creation of some age-old fairy-tale. As a boy his favourites among his mother's fireside tales had always been those that dealt with rightful heirs restored unexpectedly to their kingdoms and princesses delivered from the grim castles of ogres; and this predilection for the romance of escape, buried for years beneath the urgent practicalities of a naval career, was stirring strongly in him now.

It was increasingly irksome, he found, to be a mere auxiliary in this fascinating drama, required to push the actors onto the stage and then condemned to sit in front of a theatre curtain that never rose. Ring hadn't been enthusiastic about Captain Cockburn's resolve to exceed his orders; now he himself felt that those orders from a Government 'determined to make an effort to rescue the person of King Ferdinand the Seventh' were inadequate.

At first light the schooner sent up topsails and jibs and headed on her westerly course out through the Teignouse Passage. The light breeze on her port beam had a southerly warmth and the haze that had lain across the smooth water through the night did not entirely disperse with the coming of the sun. However, there was sufficiently good visibility to enable her to pass the narrows between the Houat islets and the Teignouse rock without hazard, and well before noon the steady following wind had taken her within gunshot of *Implacable* at the rendezvous off the Penmarch cape.

Nonpareil's longboat was called away to take the captain back to his ship. As it was being lowered Cockburn (who had occupied Ring's truckle-bed) observed that his night's sleep had been unusually sound.

'An easy conscience, Mr Ring, comes of the knowledge that you've done all that can be done in the way of duty,' he pronounced.

'Yes, sir.' Ring produced the result of his night-watch meditations. 'It's occurred to me that we might do one thing more, if you approve. When the Spaniards land I could go with them as far as the stone hut above the beach, to make certain –'

'A damned good idea, Mr Ring,' Cockburn broke in heartily. 'Make sure this Chouan feller sets off with 'em to Nantes, eh? Should have thought of it myself. Report to me immediately on your return.'

'Aye aye, sir.'

De Kolli, who looked as though a night of slow rolling in Breckinridge's berth hadn't agreed with him, was already in the longboat. The captain joined him and the boat pulled away towards the 74 that loomed dark and massive in the noonday haze. Ring was a little worried by that haze. The wind was too light to clear it and that meant it might thicken at nightfall, when *Nonpareil* would be running the Teignouse Passage on a spring tide racing in at half-flood. And to fetch an anchorage at the right spot off La Turballe, in a sea-fog at midnight, would be next to impossible. Well, there was nothing he could do about that except hope for the best.

Cockburn's orders had been to sail at four bells of the afternoon watch as before, De Kolli and Maura coming on board with their belongings half-an-hour earlier. This part of the programme duly took place and *Nonpareil* sailed on her south-easterly course with no change in wind or weather. Not until she was halfway on her forty-mile voyage did the haze begin to thicken, and with the thickening came a slight veering of the wind to west-south-west that rolled grey-white masses of fog across her bows, opening weird alleyways of open sea only to bar them next moment with impenetrable vapour. By the time Breckinridge's dead-reckoning placed them five miles north-west of the Poulains point on Belle-Ile the fog had enveloped them completely and the yielding wall of cloud into which they pushed was yellowing with the fading daylight.

Ring conferred with his second-in-command and the boatswain. Mr Lunt gave it as his opinion, based on experience, that it might clear in twenty-four hours or it might not. Breckinridge, with an anxious glance at his captain, thought their chances of getting safely through the Teignouse in present conditions were three-to-one against. This so far coincided with Ring's own assessment that he made his decision at once.

'Heave-to, Mr Breckinridge, if you please,' he said, and went below to apprise his passengers of the change in plan.

De Kolli and Maura were hunched in his cabin in earnest discussion. The Baron received the news of delay with angry consternation.

'But this leaves but the one night when we must land!' he objected. 'If for some reason we fail then, there will be no second chance, monsieur.'

Maura laid a hand on his sleeve. 'The captain is right, Baron. If we try to enter Quiberon Bay tonight the chance of failure is greater than if we wait for tomorrow. Therefore we must wait.' He turned to Ring. 'Nevertheless, monsieur, tomorrow is our last chance. You understand, I think, that the future of Spain – the freeing of His Most Catholic Majesty from the grip of the tyrant – depends on our landing tomorrow.'

'I understand.' Ring hesitated a moment. 'And I give you my word, señores, that you shall land at La Turballe tomorrow night.'

Afterwards, on deck in the fading light with the blanket of fog pressing in all round the schooner, he felt some uneasiness at that pledge; a sea-officer of his experience should have known better than to promise what the innumerable hazards of the sea might render totally impossible. It was the aura of complete dedication that surrounded Don Felicito, he thought, the fervour of purpose that emanated from him, that had led him to commit himself. But he knew that tomorrow he would fulfil his promise if it was humanly possible – even if it meant risking his ship and afterwards scouring an enemy shore in pitch darkness in search of a stone hut on a dyke above the beach.

So that night and the next morning *Nonpareil* lay like an uneasy ghost in the thick drift of sea-fog, at intervals heading westward for a short leg on port or starboard tack to maintain her approximate position off Belle-Ile. Ring was sticking to the original plan to use the last of daylight for the passage into Quiberon Bay. There was, as he knew, little sea-traffic within the Bay and there would be less in the fog; but he was not going to risk a sudden clearance in daylight revealing the schooner's presence to a chance fishing-boat, who might report it to the shore authorities. The landing had to be made on the four-mile beach between the batteries on Croisic and Castelli, and the last thing he wanted was those batteries alerted to the presence of an enemy vessel.

At four bells of the first dog-watch the fog was as thick as ever and the afternoon was darkening early. Ring dared not wait longer. De Kolli and Maura, who had been on deck for some time conversing in low voices, were politely requested to go below; with less ceremony the foredeck was cleared of idlers and the hands of the duty watch sent to stations by fore and main sheets. Ring posted Breckinridge by the helm and Buller at the wheel, Lunt and Norie to keep lookout from port and starboard rail amidships, and sent a man to the foremasthead, though up there the fog was as dense as it was at sea-level. Then he walked for'ard to the bows and kicked off his buckled shoes.

'Let her pay off!' he called to Breckinridge, and to the men at the sheets, 'Slacken away, all. Stand by to haul at my word.'

Nonpareil wore main and fore sails and inner jib. The loose canvas flapped as she turned and then bellied-out untidily as the wind came over her starboard quarter. Ring had stepped up onto the butt of the bowsprit and now was walking out along it, balancing precariously with the aid of jib and forestay. At the tack of the inner jib he lowered himself to use the rigging of the dolphin-striker for a shuffle out to the jibboom and here hauled himself up until he was standing at the tip of the spar, his stockinged feet on the narrow round of the boom and a hand grasping the taut stay of the flying jib. Eighteen feet ahead of the schooner's cutwater, he looked down on green water slowly passing astern below his toes. Gazing to his front, he saw the vague merging of wave and fog no more than a biscuit-toss away. If and when the moment came, it would demand instant action.

To have any hope of steering for the Teignouse Passage in such conditions *Nonpareil* needed a known position from which to take her departure, and her movements for the last twenty hours had left Ring and Breckinridge – despite the latter's labours with log and traverse-board – with nothing like an exact position to work from. The sum of their calculations had been that the northern point of Belle-Ile could not be more than four miles away nor less than two, and that it bore somewhere between ENE and ESE from them. Ring had ordered Breckinridge to steer the northerly course, thereby accepting the risk of sailing clean past the Pointe des Poulains without seeing it, rather than the southerly which was more likely to bring them to Belle-Ile's west coast – and more likely, too, to bring the schooner and her people to a watery grave below the savage reef-defended cliffs of that coast.

'Spill your wind, fore and main!' he shouted over his shoulder.

He wanted *Nonpareil* with as little way on her as possible but ready to use those sails when he required them. As he stared intently into the grey-white opacity ahead he recalled to his inner eye the chart's rendering of the jutting headland, a rock at the end of a sandspit with a ring of lesser rocks a quarter-mile north-west of it. Ring had marked those rocks through his glass on a previous cruise, and the pinnacle like a crooked finger that rose higher than the rest; the Poulains, the French called them – the Colts. At his first sighting of the headland (if he ever got one) he would have to go about like lightning and make away westward to get round those Colts.

Behind him the wet jib flapped sullenly. Two miles or four miles? The schooner had been heading inshore for more than twenty minutes now at three or four knots. But the tide, at half-flood, could be setting them in faster than that. He dashed accumulated fog-dew from his eyelashes and peered ahead, willing his gaze to penetrate the baffling curtain of vapour, straining his ears for the sound of wave on rock. The jibboom under his feet trembled each time the heavy sails flapped and his fingers were cramping on the jibstay. This continuous staring into nothingness was affecting his sight, making blobs and patches course across the blank of the mist. A fleck of white dead ahead was an illusion, no doubt.

A white fleck that grew and had a dark shadow behind it –

'Hard a-port! Sheets, there – haul!'

A lifetime passed before *Nonpareil* answered to helm and wind. Then she came round with a swerve and a heel that so nearly dislodged Ring from his holds that for some seconds he clung writhing and swinging like an acrobat. From the corner of his eye he saw the savage black teeth with the crooked finger of rock perched in their midst, the swirl of foam about them and the white of breaking waves. They slid past only a few yards away; only a few yards from that frail copper skin that covered her wounded side. In five seconds they were gone into the fog astern.

Ring recovered himself with a gulp. The mingling of relief and exultation that rose in him made the perilous journey back to the safety of the bows seem child's-play.

'Mr Breckinridge! Lay a course from the Poulains to the Passage, if you please.'

He hoped his voice was as calm and collected as he tried to make it. His fingers as he fumbled with his shoes were shaking uncontrollably; it had been a very near-run thing. But the positive identification of the Poulains rocks had been the best of good fortune and the chance he had taken had succeeded beyond expectation, so that he was able to regain his usual composure before walking aft. Breckinridge popped up from the companion as he reached the helm.

'East-nor'-east by east, sir,' he reported breathlessly. 'By God, sir, that was a damned close –'

'Yes, Mr Breckinridge. Course east-nor'-east by east, Buller, and steer small.'

The hazards were not finished with yet. From a starting-point five miles away *Nonpareil*, blindfold and relying on the compass, had to find the one safe opening in the long barrier of rock and islet, an opening that at this state of the tide would be hardly more than a mile wide. And the all-embracing fog was slowly darkening; in another half-hour the invisible sun would drop below the unseen horizon astern.

Ring made no alteration of sail. Wind and tide were urging the schooner eastward and she would make little leeway, but there were currents and eddies to be taken into account and it was impossible to allow for them. If she was set a half-mile to northward of her proper course she could strike on the Teignouse rock; half-a-mile to southward and she would end up a wreck on Glazic or Valhuec or another of the close rank of islets that fenced in the passage on the Houat side.

Nonpareil pushed steadily on into the insubstantial mass of vapour, the light wind just broad enough on her starboard quarter to hold steady the long booms of fore and main wide-angled out to port. Buller's experienced hand on the spokes corrected her slight deviations as the long smooth rollers lifted under her stern. Ring stood just behind him, feet apart and hands clasped behind his back; Don Felicito had come on deck again to stand silent at the rail. There was no sound but the rustle of the sails and the ceaseless hushed ripple of water at her forefoot.

The silence was broken by a low-voiced exclamation from the Spaniard. Astern of them the fog had taken on a dull russet hue and this was swiftly brightening to smoky crimson. On either hand the fog-walls broke into ragged plumes and columns which, overtaking and passing the schooner, opened corridors of dark water before her bows. The tall curves of canvas overhead glowed as with firelight, and suddenly they were looking at a long wall of red-tinted cloud receding before them across the empty plain of the sea. Fine on the port bow a splinter of black with a smudge of white at its foot broke free from the cloud-wall – the Teignouse rock; and rather closer on the starboard hand Ring could just make out the flurry of foam on the most northerly of the chain of Houat islets. *Nonpareil* was headed straight for the middle of the Teignouse Passage.

'A miracle!' Maura cried, his dark eyes shining. 'A sign, M. Ring, that the saints will be with us when we land tonight.'

'I believe you, señor,' said Ring politely; he half-believed it himself.

Astern the red eye of the sun winked finally through a narrow rift of cloud and vanished behind a black horizon. *Nonpareil* glided on in the fast-failing light, through the Passage and into the twilight waters of Quiberon Bay.

2

'I am happy that you are to land with us tonight, Monsieur Ring,' said Don Felicito. 'You share in the commencement of a mission which, to us Spaniards, is a sacred duty. The hazards and uncertainties are evident, but De Kolli and I are proud to be chosen for it – we would lay down our lives to ensure its success.'

'I trust that will not be necessary, señor,' Ring said.

The two were standing at the schooner's rail. In the darkness along the deck for'ard men were busy about preparations for lowering the cockboat. A faint glow from the companionway intensifed the darkness; De Kolli was below in the cabin packing his few necessaries into a satchel. Overhead a high cloud-ceiling hid the stars and the moon would not rise behind it for another half-hour; the onshore wind that whispered in the shrouds was light, the sea so slight that *Nonpareil* lay almost motionless to her anchor-cable. Conditions could not have been better for the business in hand, Ring told himself.

'It is like the Crusades of old,' Maura went on. 'Then the mission was to rescue the holy city from the grasp of the infidel. We go to rescue our king by divine right from the hands of the arch-tyrant, the atheist and defiler of shrines. For three years, Monsieur Ring, His Most Catholic Majesty has been a prisoner, deprived of the throne ordained for him by God.'

'King Ferdinand is a young man?' Ring asked.

'He is twenty-seven – of an age to take his rightful place as head of our nation. He is a Hapsburg, as you will know, and his father descends on the female side –'

The intricacies of descent of European monarchies had little interest for Ring and he listened with half-an-ear, his thoughts more concerned with the present than the past. In fifteen minutes' time he would embark his two passengers for the shore that lay less than two miles due east of his anchorage, invisible in the darkness, even at that distance, because of its flatness. Everything had gone smoothly – the 11-mile passage down the open waters of the Bay, the spark of light on the

Castelli point that had given him a bearing and an approximate distance, the finding of good holding-ground in eight fathoms. Since the sea was so phenomenally calm he had resolved to use the cockboat again, with Turfrey's long arms to pull it; the smaller the boat and the fewer the men involved the less danger of discovery. Not that there was much danger of that on a night like this. The schooner could not have been observed from the coast, and the chance of anyone being on those miles of deserted beach at midnight was so unlikely as to be –

'Monsieur Ring! Please to say why we shall row so long way to the shore.'

Don Felicito, evidently perceiving that he had lost his companion's attention, spoke in English as he courteously changed the subject. Ring replied in the same tongue.

'For one thing, señor, the sea's very shallow farther inshore. For another, we're on a lee shore here.'

'A lee shore? That means, perhaps, an enemy shore?'

Ring smiled in the darkness. 'It means that indeed on the Biscay coast – for Bonaparte's enemies, you understand. But for a seaman it means a shore on any coast where the wind blows the ship towards it, where if the ship becomes helpless for any reason – dismasted in a storm, or helm shot away – she's doomed to wreck herself. It's an English saying, when a man's in trouble with small hope of getting out of it, that he's on a lee shore.'

Breckinridge's voice spoke from the shadows amidships. 'Cockboat ready to launch, sir.'

'Very well, Mr Breckinridge. Lower away, if you please.' Ring peered into the obscurity. 'Where's Turfrey?'

'Here I be, sir,' drawled the invisible Turfrey.

'Over with you, then, and help the gentlemen aboard. Don Felicito, if you'll apprise the Baron de Kolli –'

'I am ready,' said De Kolli, emerging from the companion; his voice, Ring thought, trembled slightly.

The cockboat was alongside and with some aid from Breckinridge the two Spaniards got into the sternsheets, where Turfrey was heard instructing Don Felicito in his slow country drawl.

'Not there, master, so please ye. Captain, *he* has to sit there, seein' as how he'll handle the tiller. *You* sit here, d'ye see, snug in the bows –'

'Good luck, sir,' said Breckinridge.

Ring, one hand on the rail, turned to face his second-in-command. Twenty-four hours ago he had envisaged the situation if for some reason his return was long delayed – *Nonpareil* revealed at daybreak anchored here, within sight and almost within range of two enemy batteries – and had decided to insure against it. His order to that effect had been left until now so as to give Breckinridge no time for insubordinate protests.

'If I'm not back on board within two hours, Mr Breckinridge,' he said, 'you'll continue to wait until two bells of the morning watch but not a moment later. At that hour you'll up anchor, take her out through the Passage, and report on board *Implacable* off the Penmarch at the earliest opportunity. Is that clear?'

'Y-yes, sir – but sir, I can't leave –'

'Those are my orders, Mr Breckinridge,' said Ring sternly, and stepped down into the boat.

Turfrey shoved-off deftly and before he had made a dozen strokes the schooner had merged with the darkness astern. The shore ahead was equally invisible, but the wind, which was blowing dead onshore, and the run of the small waves moving in towards the beach, were sufficient guides for Ring's steering for the moment. He could only guess at *Nonpareil*'s position relative to the long curve of the La Turballe beach (an informed guess, for he had been at pains to anchor according to a careful estimate) and he would have to try and identify the place of rendezvous by sight; if, indeed, there was anything to see.

He pictured the chart and Jeanne Bonchamps' pointing finger – a slim finger but brown as any fisherman's – indicating the site of the stone hut. *On the grass dyke to the south of the marsh,* she had said. A dyke shouldn't be hard to recognise even in the dark; and the hut a hundred paces beyond high-water mark. Not many women, he reflected, could have been so clear and concise in giving that sort of direction – but then Jeanne was not like any woman he had ever known. What reason could she have for landing on this beach? Business connected with De

Feriet's smuggling trade, perhaps. The man had said she was his partner –

'Listen!' De Kolli, beside him on the stern thwart, spoke suddenly. 'I hear the noise of waves.'

It was the beat and rush of surf not far ahead; not a dangerous surf, Ring thought.

'We approach the shore,' he said. 'I and the seaman will get out and pull the boat up as far as we can. Then you will have to get your feet wet, I'm afraid.' As he spoke he was stooping low over the tiller to stare ahead. 'From now on, señores,' he added, 'we should be silent.'

The irregular black crests now visible against the faintly luminous sky must be the dunes between foreshore and marsh. Nothing resembling a dyke. Turfrey's short strong pulls brought them closer in, the white line of the surf showed below the dunes, and Ring's gaze moving far to the right picked up a straight edge among the dune crests like the roof-ridge of a house. He put the tiller over to port and the boat turned parallel to the shoreline, wallowing in the troughs of waves gathering impetus before their final destruction. Five minutes' pulling and the black rim could be seen as the seaward end of a dyke running inland from the dunes, with the shape of a small building breaking its level outline. Ring swung the tiller again, heading straight for the shore.

Turfrey's oars scraped bottom as they rose and fell across the white turmoil but the surge of waves bore them onward. The forefoot ground into sand below the sliding foam. Ring and Turfrey sprang overboard to drag boat and Spaniards a few yards farther until De Kolli and Maura could climb out to splash through ankle-deep water to the dry sand of the beach.

The low mounds of the dunes, dark with marram-grass, rose a stone's-throw away with the butt-end of the dyke like a flat-topped obelisk standing slightly higher and a little to the right. The hut was out of sight from this angle but Ring could make out the pale line of a narrow path ascending the flank of the dyke in its direction. Beside him the Spaniards were settling the satchels on their shoulders. De Kolli raised an arm, pointing to the path, and set off towards it at a surprising speed for a man of his build, with Maura close behind him. Ring was about to follow when Turfrey's hand caught his sleeve and

Turfrey's voice spoke in his ear.

'Beg parding, sir – there's folk up yonder. I see the blink of a glim when we was haulin' the boat –'

'Quiet, damn you!' Ring whispered angrily. 'Stay here by the boat.'

His own fault; he should have told the man what to expect. He started up the soft sand after the Spaniards, conscious of anxiety relieved. There had always been doubt in his mind that this tryst would be kept by the other parties to the plan and that doubt was now resolved. The Chouan had been rash to show a light, but that could mean that he had no fear of discovery. His feet sank in the muddy ooze of a streamlet as he reached the start of the path. The stream issued from a reed-filled ditch that ran below the dyke's steep embankment, between it and the half-seen bulk of the dunes on his left, and when he had taken a few paces up the rough path mounting above it he could sense rather than see the wide expanse of salt-marsh stretching inland behind the dunes. The muffled beat of the surf behind him, the constant rustle of wind in the reeds below, were the only sounds.

Ring was halfway up the path, and the Spaniards a dozen yards ahead had just reached the crest, when he became aware of someone treading close behind him. Turfrey, by God – disobeying his orders! He halted and turned. And in that instant night and silence were shattered as if by the explosion of a petard. A clamour of shouts burst out above him, lights flashed and flickered, and before he could grasp what was happening he was seized from behind in an iron clasp and swung off the path. Down he went, still fast held, to land with a thump that knocked breath and sense out of him in the mud under the tall reeds of the ditch. His dazed mind retained a single word, the warning screech Maura had given: '*Trahi!*'

The heavy body that was lying across him moved cautiously to a less irksome position and Turfrey, his lips tickling Ring's ear, spoke in a hoarse whisper.

'Lie quiet, sir – the Frenchies have got 'em.'

Betrayed. Fools they had been to trust De Feriet! He was about to move when a harsh voice spoke from the darkness close overhead.

'Set him on his feet, *imbécile*! Tie his hands behind him, and

the other. – Corporal! Take six men and get down to the beach.
Patrol it in both directions. Fire if you see anything move.'

Heavy footsteps pounded down the path a dozen feet above.
Ring was glad enough to lie still though Turfrey's elbow was
boring into his stomach and water was soaking such of his
clothing as was not already wet from the surf. His shaken
senses were fast returning. The officer up there would probably
assume that the Spaniards had been landed from a ship's boat
which had immediately pulled away again – but the corporal
and his men could scarcely miss the cockboat. As the thought
crossed his mind shouts sounded distantly from the beach and
the harsh voice answered.

'Render it useless, then! Knock a hole in the bottom – use
your musket-butts!'

The noise of splintering blows told of the cockboat's end as a
means of escape. *Nonpareil*'s boat – his boat! Illogically, it was
this quite warrantable precaution on the part of the French
that set light to Ring's anger, with him a slow-burning
combustible apt to end in an explosion. Somehow he would
make them pay for it! But just now there were more pressing
questions. Would the officer guess that the boat had held more
than two? Common sense should tell him that two foreign
agents landing on enemy soil wouldn't leave their boat lying
about to be discovered. A brief search would reveal them down
here in the ditch – and the night was less dark than it had been;
behind the canopy of cloud the moon was rising.

The voices and trampling of feet up above sounded
uncomfortably close. He hoped his white breeches were
sufficiently muddied to make them invisible under the screen
of reeds. The glow of a lantern outlined the rim overhead and
the officer shouted orders to the men on the beach: they were
to remain on patrol until daybreak and then report to him at
Le Croisic. The harsh voice came again, sharply.

'*Esconade, formez*! – Prisoners in the middle – March!'

A solid tramping of boots began, slowly receding. By raising
his head Ring could see the swaying nimbus of lantern-light
moving steadily away along the crest of the dyke. There was a
good track up there, then, doubtless leading to the fort at Le
Croisic, whence De Kolli and Maura would in due course be
taken to Nantes. Wild thoughts of attempting a rescue raced

through his mind, to be quickly dismissed. A squad of soldiers armed with muskets – what could he and Turfrey hope to do against them, unarmed, ignorant of the terrain, retreat cut off? To abandon the Spaniards to their fate seemed a coward's act but they could do no other. Their own position, with an armed patrol between them and the sea, was sufficiently hazardous. It was also damned uncomfortable.

'Out of here,' he growled, writhing clear of Turfrey. 'Into the dunes yonder.'

The big seaman crawled ahead of him on hands and knees, parting the close stems of the reeds to reach a slant of mud that rose to sandy turf at the base of a dune that loomed straight in front. The light wind stirring the tufts of marram-grass bore to their ears the distant voices of the soldiers on the beach to their left, and without pausing Turfrey led to the right round the landward slope of the dune. The invisible moon behind the clouds shed light enough for them to see their footing, dimly revealing the strange cell-like pattern etched in white on the flat grey expanse that spread away inland – the salt-pans, Ring remembered. Feet sliding in the steeply-angled sand, he followed Turfrey round a projecting ridge of the dune beyond which was a bay or hollow. On the corner the seaman came to a sudden halt.

'Someone ahead of us, sir,' he muttered.

They stood motionless, listening. Above the sibilation of the wind there came to Ring's ear a sound he couldn't identify; it might almost have been a person sobbing. He stepped past Turfrey and challenged.

'*Qui vive?*'

The sound stopped instantly. In the brief pause he heard an unmistakable sniff. A small shape rose from the sand where it had been crouching and took a step forward.

'It is I, Monsieur Ring,' said Jeanne Bonchamps.

2

Ring's first reaction was suspicion. Here was De Feriet's 'partner' on the scene of De Feriet's treachery.

'What are you doing here?' he demanded sharply.

'I came to watch, monsieur, to prove my doubts unfounded. I couldn't believe that he – that Yves –'

She choked on the name and for a moment Ring thought she was going to burst into weeping. In the dim light he could make out nothing of her features, only that she was bareheaded and dressed in the seaman's jacket and trousers of their first meeting. She controlled herself quickly.

'I don't know why you came ashore with them but you are in grave peril. Your boat is stove-in –'

'I know it, mademoiselle,' Ring said between his teeth.

'– and there are seven soldiers on the beach.' She was speaking fast and urgently. 'We must get to my boat – I can take you to your ship.'

The girl would have sailed across from Houat, of course. 'Where is your boat?' he asked.

'Not five minutes from here if we hurry. Come!'

Without waiting for a reply she started round the slope of the dune. Ring threw a word of explanation over his shoulder as he followed.

'All's well, Turfrey – mademoiselle's got a boat.'

'Let's hope you're right, sir,' Turfrey grunted doubtfully.

Jeanne led them at a pace that kept both men at full stretch, contouring the shoulders of the dunes, clambering through miniature cols between ridges fledged with marram-grass, once dropping to a narrow gully where water from the salt-marsh drained through to the shore. Ring, toiling behind her with no need to give thought to his route, felt the fire of anger rising in him. It was fuelled not so much by De Feriet's faithlessness as by the ease with which the mission to Valençay had been disabled before it had really begun. De Kolli and Maura, Captain Cockburn, Robert Ring, and the British Government itself – all had been made fools of by Fortune. And he, Ring, had been made to look the biggest fool of all. He had been entrusted with the safe landing of two Spanish agents on the coast of France, and what had he done? He had put them straight into the hands of the Emperor's soldiers; had been deprived of his boat, rolled into a ditch, and finally enabled to sneak back on board his ship only because of a lucky meeting with a French girl. A king's freedom, a nation's future – even, perhaps, victory or defeat in the war in Spain – had depended on the success of this mission, and now it would never –

'*Attention!*' Jeanne's low-voiced warning halted them. 'My boat is just beyond here – we must cross the beach swiftly.'

They had come sliding down into another of the flat-bottomed gullies through which the sea reached the salt-marsh at spring tides. It wound through the narrow belt of dunes a few hundred yards north of the dyke, and they had reached it just short of where it opened onto the beach. A bend of the gully hid this opening from them, but the murmur of the surf came very clearly to their ears. Jeanne's boat would be high and dry now that the ebb was running, Ring reflected, but he and Turfrey would be able to drag it into the water. He could feel no elation at the near prospect of escape, however; to return safely, leaving a botched job behind him, was a crime according to his calendar.

Treading the level sand of the gully floor with its shallow rivulets, they came in single file to the bend and saw the beach before them – and the boat, a hundred yards away. And the three men walking towards it.

Jeanne had stopped on the instant, pressed against the sandy wall of the gully. Ring, so close behind her that he could feel her body's warmth, peered over her head to see this ruin of their hopes. Boat and soldiers were black shapes on a grey background but the gestures of the men and their half-heard dialogue made the little drama clear. First they inspected the boat, one climbing into her canted hull and out again. Then another – the corporal, Ring thought – gave a peremptory order to which his subordinates plainly objected. The corporal shouted their objections down with a stream of oaths and much gesticulation towards the boat. Ring guessed he was repeating his officer's orders concerning the cockboat: this boat too was to be rendered useless.

The girl had realised their purpose – he felt her make a convulsive movement as if she was going to spring forward, and laid a hand on her arm to restrain her. He could sympathise with her feelings; the poor wench had lost her faith in her protector and now she was going to lose her boat. And that boat might be his and Turfrey's last chance.

Likely enough the soldiers had been arguing that this was a fisherman's boat and nothing to do with the landing of the

Spaniards; if so, their corporal's vehemence overruled them. They unslung their muskets and began to batter half-heartedly at the boat's planking, at first with so little effect, this being a heavier boat than *Nonpareil*'s cockboat, that the corporal was incensed. He pushed them violently aside and launched a kick at the hull to show how easily it could be done. His subsequent eloquence as he danced about trying to rub his foot with one hand while supporting himself on his musket with the other far outdid his previous effort.

This was the moment Ring had been waiting for. Those muskets could not be loaded, and he and Turfrey would cover the hundred yards before powder and bullet could be got down their barrels. He was on the point of giving the order to break cover when a distant shout coming from the unseen beach to his left made him pause. It was as well that he did so. Almost at once the remaining four men of the patrol came into sight advancing towards the others. Two against seven – and what would happen to Jeanne if so desperate an attack failed? No, it wouldn't do.

The newcomers were quickly thrown into the assault on the boat. The racket of half-a-dozen musket-butts crashing on the planking woke a melancholy protest from some seagulls farther along the dunes, and in half-a-minute the chorus was augmented by screeches of triumph. The boat was stove-in. The watchers in the gully knew themselves marooned on a hostile coast. Jeanne turned without a word and the three retreated until they all stood in the cover of the gully's bend.

'I am sorry.' The girl's voice was low but steady. 'After all, I am no help to you. What shall we do?'

Turfrey spoke. 'So please ye, sir, we'd best move, an' quickish too. If they Frenchies mind to come lookin' –'

'You're right,' Ring said, thinking fast. 'Mademoiselle, we must talk – but not here.'

'I know a place,' Jeanne said at once. 'It is half a league from here but we can be safe there while the darkness lasts. Shall I lead you there?'

'If you please.'

Behind them as they went back along the gully the voices of the men on the beach diminished and passed out of hearing. Jeanne led them through the break in the dunes and out to the brink of the marsh, turning to the left across the landward slopes without hesitation, as one familiar with the way. Ring, following with Turfrey trotting at his heels, was conscious of the indeterminate spaces of the salt-marsh on his right hand but was too occupied with his own thoughts to give much heed to their route. There was no hope now of getting back to *Nonpareil*. Breckinridge would up anchor in a few hours' time and he and Turfrey would be reported taken or dead; as indeed they might be in fact, before many hours had passed. But the fire that had smouldered within Robert Ring during this last crowded half-hour burned now with a clear and rising flame – not of anger but of dogged resolution. The mission that had so taken hold on his imagination hadn't yet failed entirely. De Kolli and Maura were out of it but he was not, and he could pass as a Frenchman better than any Spanish Agent. The difficulties that would confront him – and they were enormous – were no greater than those that would have confronted the Spaniards, he told himself, and from what he had seen of them he was better capable of facing them than they were.

To bolster these arguments came other thoughts. He had blamed Fortune for tonight's reverses but that was to shy away from the truth. He, Ring, had sowed the seeds of failure – had condoned the enlistment of De Feriet – had lacked the sense to reconnoitre the stone hut before ushering his charges into the hands of the enemy; and he was still free and capable of action. It was his plain duty to press forward with the plan to the limit of his ability. And, by God, he would do so!

He was suddenly aware that they had turned away from the dunes and were threading a way between clumps of gorse on a turfy slope. Jeanne stopped beside a large gorse-bush below which the ground sank in a grassy hollow.

'*Nous voici*,' she said a little wearily, and sank down on the turf. 'I am at home, monsieur, for I've often rested here on my way to Guérande.'

Ring sat himself down in the hollow with Turfrey squatting a few feet away. 'Guérande?' he repeated. 'We are near a town, then?'

'A very little town. By the path above this place one may reach it in twenty minutes. Yves –' she checked herself and then went on quickly. 'Monsieur de Feriet had much business with the *maire*, Monsieur Godinot.'

'Ah. Now tell me this, mademoiselle, if you please. Did you know that Monsieur de Feriet was to betray us?'

'No!' The girl almost shouted the word. 'You must not think that!'

In the darkness he couldn't see her face but he knew that she was struggling to control herself. After a pause she began to speak, rapidly and in a flat expressionless tone. For a long time now she had feared that De Feriet's thirst for money-making had supplanted his old enthusiasm for the royalist cause. Perceiving this, he had taken to teasing her about it, telling her gravely that he would sell King Louis himself if the price was high enough and then roaring with laughter at her dismay. Jeanne had come to accept this as his idea of humour; but the conference on board the lugger at Port Halai had renewed her doubts.

'The Spaniard's mention of Valençay told us the real objective,' she said. 'There have been hints and rumours – among the Chouans, you understand – of some attempt to be made to rescue the King of Spain. For me this would be a splendid enterprise, but for Yves – I saw from his face that he was weighing the worth of the secret in gold.'

After the lugger had sailed that night she had been unable to quiet her suspicions. The night of fog, when she had lain wondering whether the landing would be attempted in spite of the conditions, had left her more uneasy than ever. Next day she had resolved that these doubts could only be laid to rest by assuring herself that the Spaniards landed safely; and so she had sailed from Houat at sunset to conceal herself in the dunes and to watch – to watch –

Here her self-possession gave way and she ended in an outburst of sobbing. Ring, somewhat at a loss, groped for her hand and patted it soothingly.

'I'm very sorry, mademoiselle,' he said gruffly. 'But – this is now past and we must look to the future. The Monsieur Godinot you speak of at Guérande – will he help you if you go to him?'

He heard her gulp down her emotion. 'I can be sure of his help. He was once among the most active Chouans. But he is an old man now and a *maire* – he won't want to know anything about this night's doings. I can't ask him to hide two Englishmen from the authorities.'

'Nor would I ask him to. I thought that Godinot might be able to arrange for you to return to Houat –'

'And to Yves?' she flashed at him angrily. '*Jamais de la vie*, Monsieur Ring! Please understand that all that is finished for me now.'

'Then what will you do?'

'I don't know,' she said indifferently. 'Something – I've many friends among the Chouans. But for you it is different. Have you any plan?'

Ring hesitated a moment, then decided he had no alternative but to tell her.

'Yes, mademoiselle. I and Turfrey are going to make our way to Valençay. We shall bring away King Ferdinand if we can.'

She drew in her breath sharply. '*Mais – dieu-de-dieu*, monsieur, that is madness! It is impossible that you should succeed.'

'Nevertheless, we shall try.'

'Reflect a little – only a little!' she said urgently; her own troubles seemed forgotten. 'You are in the dress of an English officer, your man here speaks no French, you have no money – or perhaps you have money?'

'No,' Ring admitted.

'*Tiens*! You would be arrested before you had gone a league on this mad journey.'

Jeanne paused for a long moment. When she spoke again her voice held a new note, a tone in which excitement and – oddly – a trace of merriment were blended.

'Unless,' she said slowly, 'I come with you, monsieur.'

'You?' Ring was startled into brusqueness. 'It's not to be thought of, mademoiselle. I could not allow you –'

'Allow?' she repeated mockingly. 'I think you forget, Monsieur Ring, that France is my country, not yours. Also –' she was suddenly serious – 'you have shown me how I may make some amends for – for Yves. Indeed, if you will not take me as your comrade I shall journey to Valençay by myself.'

'That would be foolish,' he said abruptly. 'Are not you

yourself a proscribed person in France?'

'I can find means to travel nevertheless. Listen, monsieur.' Her hand came firmly down on his knee. 'We make a compact here and now – you and I and this man whose name I don't know – to join in carrying out this enterprise. I can help you, you see. I can find money and clothes for our needs, to start with, before dawn.'

'But –'

'Old Godinot was in the army of La Vendée,' she hurried on, 'and now he is banker for – for us of Houat. I must see him now.'

'At this hour?'

'It's the hour of my usual visit, though not the day. Monsieur Ring –' her fingers tightened on his knee – 'you must take me with you. Indeed,' she added with what might have been the ghost of a laugh, 'I think you have no choice.'

Ring knew she was right. He was more than a little puzzled by the swiftness with which Jeanne could change from a weeping girl to a quick-witted enthusiast in a new project; but if she could indeed provide the help she promised it would make the difference between a thin chance and no chance at all. And if his desperate scheme had to be saddled with a woman, better this one than another. He put his hand on hers.

'I agree,' he said briefly.

'*Bien.*' She slipped her hand free and stood up. 'Again you must follow me, *Monsieur le capitaine du vaisseau.* Tomorrow you shall take command.'

Ring turned to where Abel Turfrey crouched silent in the obscurity, ignorant of what momentous decisions were being taken.

'Turfrey,' he said, 'we're going to make a journey into France and mademoiselle is coming with us. At the end of it we're going to free the King of Spain from the castle where Boney's got him caged-up. What d'you say to that?'

The three-second pause before Turfrey answered was the only token of his surprise at this sudden and unlikely proposition.

'If so be as that's an order, sir,' he returned impassively, 'the answer's "aye aye, sir". If it's an invite, like, I'm main happy to accept.'

In the darkness Ring smiled for the first time that night. 'Come on, then,' he said.

Two minutes later they were once more following Jeanne through the darkness, on a little path that wound through the gorse-bushes towards Guérande.

V

The Road to Valençay

1

The strident crowing of a cock woke Ring. For a moment he was a boy again in Redon with his mother, talking and thinking in French, laughing at the notice in a *cabaret* with its crude drawing of a cock and the legend beneath it – *Quand ce coq chantera Ici crédit l'on fera.* Then he was wide awake and instantaneously aware of his situation.

Grey morning light filtered through the rough plank wall of the barn where he was lying half buried in straw. From a few feet away came Turfrey's muffled snoring. Jeanne had found this refuge, the property of Godinot the *maire* of Guérande, and had left them there to await her return before sunrise; she herself had gone on into the sleeping town to find Monsieur Godinot and get from him what help she could.

So far as Ring had been able to discern in the obscurity, Guérande was a compact little town perched on a plateau above the marshes, its houses huddled within a ring of ancient ramparts below which an untidy congeries of huts, barns and plots of cultivation spread down to the lower levels. Monsieur Godinot's barn was on the east side, close below the ramparts where a rough track issued from the town, and to reach it they had threaded a precarious way round the cabbage-patches and past byres where cattle and horses stirred and snorted at their passing. Jeanne had hardly left them before both men, burrowing into the straw, were asleep.

Ring, sitting up and stretching stiffened limbs, reflected that for the moment all the onus of this reckless enterprise (how reckless he was not just now prepared to consider) lay upon Jeanne; they were entirely dependent upon her, and he was a little surprised to find that his trust in her was absolute. He cautiously pushed open the rickety door of the barn and stepped outside to relieve himself. The morning was still dark and he could make out little beyond the rampart wall rising above, a raft of mist lying over the marsh below, and a wooden trough into which a spring below the ramparts discharged its water by way of a hollowed treetrunk. He splashed icy water over his face and was ready to face the pressing problems of the immediate future.

The first of these was the question of pursuit. Ring could not doubt that there would be one. The French officer in charge of last night's ambush was a fool; he should have searched the neighbourhood of the stone hut as soon as the discovery of the cockboat indicated that others beside the two Spaniards had landed. De Feriet would have told the authorities in Nantes that the landing was to be made from a British warship and the plain implication of the cockboat was that one, if not two, members of His Majesty's Navy were on shore.

De Feriet, however, had not known of Ring's decision to accompany De Kolli and Maura to the rendezvous; and perhaps the officer was of the sort that stuck to the bare letter of his orders, which would be to catch two Spanish agents and bring them to Nantes. When he made his report, though, someone would perceive or suspect the truth. De Feriet would guess it, for one. But then De Feriet was *persona non grata* in Nantes – 'even in Nantes I must never be seen and recognised,' he had said – and therefore, having presumably lodged his information by some indirect channel, could take no steps to direct a pursuit. Would he hear of the second boat on the beach, and guess that Jeanne Bonchamps was with them? Unlikely, perhaps; and in any case it would be some time before Jeanne's boat was identified. Search and pursuit would be set in motion well before that if there was an intelligent commander in Nantes, and since prisoners and escort would certainly reach Nantes within the next twelve hours there might be a squadron of *chasseurs* hunting through the sand dunes and riding into Guérande before sunset.

Across the half-seen flats to eastward the sky was paling and already there was the faintest tinge of pink on the clouded horizon. A hundred and fifty miles beyond that horizon lay

Valençay, whither he proposed to go for the purpose of stealing a King of Spain from under the noses of his keepers. If there was any awareness in Robert Ring's mind that this proposition was folly of the first magnitude, its achievement a possibility so unlikely as to be absurd, he refused to consider it. His decision was made and the only questions to be answered concerned the means of getting to Valençay.

Ring had thought of this journey as a secret progress by way of the wild tracts and forests between the towns and villages, seeking refuge and food with Chouan sympathisers. But now that he had admitted the probability of pursuit he saw that speed, not secrecy, was the key to escape. It might take them weeks to creep across the country through thickets and marshes, and if there was some Frenchman perspicacious enough to guess what they were up to – and De Feriet might, for instance – the news would reach Valençay long before them. It was highly improbable that the French hereabouts had a chain of semaphores like the one linking London and Portsmouth, so news could travel no faster than the speed of a horse. Somehow they must travel faster than the news.

There was the problem of equipment for an overland journey, too – clothing and shoes. The buckled shoes he was wearing were well enough for a deck but would soon fall to pieces on a cross-country journey; Turfrey had on a pair of canvas slippers soled with rope, of his own construction. Ring glanced down at his once-white breeches. They had dried on him overnight but the half-light showed them stained and caked with mud, like his blue coat. Even so, they marked him for a British naval officer, and Turfrey's outfit of canvas smock and loose trousers, though less conspicuous, was not what a Breton peasant would wear. The solution depended – he disliked the thought – upon Jeanne.

And there was Turfrey himself, unable to speak or understand French. There was only one way round that – and as he thought of it there came the sound of a muffled sneeze from the barn. Ring went in and bade the dimly-visible figure that confronted him a brisk good-morning. The response was a horrible croaking noise. Turfrey seemed to be gesturing, pointing with hands to his ears and then to his mouth.

'What the devil –' began Ring, and stopped with a chuckle.

'So you've tumbled to it, have you?'

''Tis the only way, sir, I reckon,' Turfrey said apologetically. 'Deef an' dumb for me, if I'm not to be smoked by the first Frenchy as tries to get me talkin'. I could be a natural too, sir, a looby, if so be's you thought it a good idee. I've tried it afore.'

'No. Stick to deaf and dumb and no more. When did you try it before?'

'When I was up in front of the justices, sir, for takin' Squire Olifant's game.'

'Did it succeed?'

''Twould ha' worked like a charm, sir, but that Keeper Willetts, who'd known me since I was a lad –' Turfrey stopped dead. 'Someone's up betimes,' he muttered. 'Comin' this way, sir.'

He stepped to the barn door which Ring had left ajar and closed it noiselessly. Ring heard, now, the sound of footsteps and the grating rattle of a wheel on the rough track coming from the town. He touched Turfrey's arm and they drew back into the darkness of the barn and crouched behind the straw. The sounds came quickly nearer down the hill, accompanied by the tune of *Auprès de ma blonde* whistled in a low key. The truck or wheelbarrow bumped to a halt close to their door. Something thumped against the wooden wall and a man's voice growled curtly.

'*Dedans! Pour vous.*'

The whistling began again and receded with the footsteps and the sound of the wheel. Ring waited until they were out of hearing and then brought in the object that had been left for them. It was a large leather shoulder-pack of the sort carried by pedlars, bulging and heavy, and he examined its contents by the growing light that came in through the half-open door. A round black hat and a red knitted woollen cap; two coats and two pairs of breeches; two pairs of stout-soled shoes; a bottle of wine and a cloth bag containing bread and meat; and a worn case which proved to hold a pair of razors. Ring hadn't realised how hungry he was until he saw their prospective breakfast, but it was the razors that roused his admiration. What a girl she was! Jeanne's choice of the minimum essentials (he hoped they would fit) couldn't have been bettered and this extra, which might be called an essential luxury, showed unusual forethought. Turfrey, who had watched the unpacking from a respectful distance, voiced his commander's opinion for him.

'By hookey, sir, that's a rare lass, that mamzelle of yours!'

'She's rare but she's not mine,' Ring said briefly. 'Breakfast first. Then we'll rig ourselves.'

He divided the bread and meat into two equal portions and they fell to, taking turn about at the wine-bottle and wasting no time in talk. The roseate tint on the eastern clouds had brightened to gold and Ring knew that sunrise could not be more than half-an-hour away.

As soon as they had finished making short work of the meal he sorted out the clothes, while Turfrey washed himself at the trough. The two suits had obviously belonged to a man somewhat taller than Ring and the shoes were a size larger than his, but they would do. The coat and breeches of dark grey broadcloth he apportioned to himself and the other suit, of coarser brown cloth, to Turfrey. The black hat fitted him well enough, his shirt and stock were still presentable, and when he had scraped most of the mud off his white stockings and was arrayed in the grey suit he felt he could pass a not-too-close inspection; as a petty official, perhaps – as his half-formed plan prompted. Turfrey, with his massive shoulders nearly splitting the seams of the brown coat, had only his seaman's smock to wear beneath it and showed a good deal of hairy chest, but looked the part of a servant and factotum of the rougher sort.

In Ring's mind, as he rolled their discarded clothing into a bundle, was the knowledge that he had crossed a Rubicon. Capture in naval uniform meant at least the chance of life, at best a short imprisonment before exchange and repatriation. Capture in diguise meant death as a spy. He pushed the bundle under a heap of rotting harness and other rubbish in the far corner of the barn and they sat down on the straw to wait for Jeanne.

The life of Guérande was beginning to stir. A voice called distantly and was answered, up in the little town above the ramparts. Nearer at hand a cow lowed repeatedly and urgently, and the radiance of the still-unrisen sun was lightening the dark corners of the barn. Ring was repressing a rising anxiety when – without a sound to herald her coming – Jeanne slipped in through the door and stood before them. She was dressed in a full-skirted gown of some russet material with a small straw bonnet perched on her neatly-braided hair, and carried three cloaks on her arm.

'You are dressed and ready – that is good,' she said breathlessly. 'And you have slept?' she added as they got to their feet.

Ring made her a bow. 'We have, mademoiselle – and I see that you have, too. You look like Aurora herself.'

The compliment was sincere. Jeanne's face was eager and smiling like a pretty child's, and her brown eyes were bright with excitement. She coloured slightly under his regard.

'Madame Godinot made me sleep for an hour or two,' she said. 'She has been very kind – and Monsieur Godinot too. Those clothes you have on belonged to his son who was conscripted into the army in the spring. They're too fine for our purpose but they could find me no others.'

'For my purpose,' said Ring, 'they couldn't be better.'

Jeanne shot a puzzled glance at him. 'They're too good for rough travel. The brown coat,' she added, eyeing it critically, 'looks as if it won't last long on your man, whose name I don't know –'

'I beg your pardon, mademoiselle.' He waved a hand in introduction. 'Seaman Turfrey – Mademoiselle Jeanne Bonchamps.' Jeanne took a step backwards as Turfrey, opening his mouth and pointing to it, uttered his inarticulate croak. 'But from this moment,' Ring went on, 'he's our servant Antoine – deaf and dumb, poor fellow.'

She smiled. 'Ah – I understand. And I'll remember. But we mustn't linger here. Godinot doesn't want you to enter his town but has agreed to another plan. First, though, I must give you this.'

From beneath the cloaks on her arm she took a small leather bag and handed it to Ring. It was heavy for its size and when he had untied the fastening cord he saw that it contained money, silver francs of the Imperial mint and gold 'napoleons,' twenty-franc pieces. For what he had in mind there was more than enough.

'That is Monsieur de Feriet's money,' Jeanne was saying, a

touch of defiance in her voice. 'I told Godinot the clothes and the money were urgently needed for a secret project against Bonaparte – which was true. I told him Yves had said it was safer for him to know nothing of it – which was a lie. You don't think it was stealing?' she added anxiously.

Ring slipped the leather bag into a pocket of his borrowed coat. 'Mademoiselle,' he said slowly, 'I think you are *la fée marraine* of the old story, a worker of magic. Thanks to you, we're clothed and shod and fed, with money for our needs. I don't know anyone who could have done so well.'

She reddened at his praise and the admiration in his glance. 'We are comrades, are we not?' she said in a low voice. 'I must try to do my share.'

'You've done more than that. But –' Ring spoke more lightly – 'I've not thanked you for the razors. I'll use them at the first opportunity.'

Jeanne laughed. 'A man is not a man until he has shaved. That was what Yves used to –' She stopped suddenly, frowning. 'But we have a rendezvous and our time is short. Quickly, now – I'll tell you as we go.' She rolled the cloaks and thrust them into the leather pack. 'Antoine will carry it?' she asked Ring.

'Yes. Turfrey –' Ring checked himself and gestured.

Turfrey slung the pack on his shoulders. Ring went to the door, opened it cautiously to look out, and nodded to the others. The rim of the sun dazzled above the mist-wreathed marsh as they emerged into the brisk morning air. Jeanne accepted Ring's proffered arm with a smile, and with Turfrey trudging behind they began to follow a narrow track that wound across the slope below the walls of Guérande, twisting round the wooden sheds and patches of cultivation.

There were people about now: two men and a woman working in a cabbage-patch below the path, a two-horse wagon moving slowly along the verge of the marsh lower down, a man with a spade on his shoulder coming towards them down the path. Ring spoke a casual '*bon matin*' to the spade-bearer as he passed them and received a gruff reply. Glancing back over his shoulder, he saw the man pause and turn to look after them and then go on his way. After all, he told himself, there was nothing very remarkable about them except that they were strangers; in a small place like Guérande an unfamiliar face would of course be noticed, but he doubted whether a Breton peasant would trouble his head about how they came to be here. All the same, they were leaving a trail that could be followed.

As they went unhurriedly on Jeanne explained what she had arranged with Godinot. The *maire*, who had extensive vegetable fields, was to despatch one of his carts with some sacks of cabbages for the market-town of Pontchâteau three leagues away. The cart would leave the Place St Aubin at sunrise and pick them up on the Pontchâteau road to carry them to a point beyond La Chapelle where they would take to their feet, leaving the road.

'We shall travel secretly from there,' she told Ring. 'First through the Forest of Gavre – I know the paths, and I can find friends, good Chouans, who will shelter us. Then –'

'No.'

At Ring's curt interruption Jeanne glanced quickly up at him, but her question was forestalled by their arrival on the road. The path they had followed had joined the road, which was no better than a broad rutted track, some distance from the town entrance and at the junction three country fellows were standing in talk. One of them touched his battered hat to Jeanne and gave them a cheerful good-morning.

Ring nodded in response. '*Fait beau temps, eh?*'

'*Je crois. Pas de pluie aujourd'hui. Bonne promenade!*'

They walked on, away from the town. Turning, Ring saw the three men once more absorbed in conversation and beyond them, just emerging from the town entrance, a hooded tumbril drawn by a single horse.

'Are all the roads in these parts as bad as this one?' he asked Jeanne abruptly.

'Oh, no.' She answered without hesitation, though her brow was creased in a frown. 'At Pontchâteau the new road begins. It's one of Bonaparte's *routes nationales*, as he calls them, and goes all the way to Angers and beyond.'

'To Tours? And Blois?'

'I think it does. But surely you're not –'

'Listen, mademoiselle. We've no time to seek out your Chouan friends and to do so might be dangerous. We don't know how much De Feriet has told the authorities in Nantes.'

He felt her wince at that. 'Monsieur Godinot's man with the cabbages will be up with us in a moment,' he went on quickly. 'He shall take us right to Pontchâteau. From there we'll journey like ordinary travellers – except that the money you brought will grease our wheels.'

'But we have no papers! Monsieur, the risk is too –'

'I am – let me see – Robert Bague, in the service of the Department of Viticulture,' Ring pursued unheeding. 'I travel with Madame Bague and our servant and I'm commissioned to inspect the *vignobles* of the Pays du Loire for phylloxera.' He grinned at her astonished face. 'I'm the son of a vintner, you know.'

Jeanne's hand on his arm gripped it tightly. 'It's madness. That way we invite discovery.'

'Rather we outdistance it, mademoiselle. The man Robespierre sent to the guillotine for his honesty shall give us our watchword – *de l'audace, encore de l'audace, toujours de l'audace!*'

'But –'

'Let me remind you, mademoiselle, that last night you told me that today I would be in command.'

Jeanne was silent for a moment. The wheels of the approaching cart creaked and rumbled closed behind them. Then –

'We shall have to stay at inns,' she said thoughtfully. 'It would be more – more *convenable* if I were Mademoiselle Bague your sister, monsieur.'

Ring, who was not given to blushing, did so now.

'*Soit*,' he said hastily. 'Forgive me, mademoiselle I had not thought –'

He was glad to cut short his stammered apologies by steering Jeanne out of the way of the hooded tumbril, which had pulled up alongside. The driver was an old man with a clay pipe gripped between toothless gums. Without a word he jerked his thumb towards the back of the cart. Ring made gestures at Turfrey, who climbed in and helped Jeanne up, and scrambled aboard after them. They settled themselves as best they could among the sacks of cabbages and the tumbril creaked into motion, trundling into the eye of the risen sun along the road for Pontchâteau. The sunlight filtering through the dingy hood showed Jeanne smiling; but suddenly her face was grave, even severe.

'Robert,' she said accusingly, 'your white stockings are a perfect disgrace. You will give them to me tonight and I will wash them.'

2

Monsieur Godinot's tumbril, pulled by a strong young mare, could better four miles in the hour on a reasonable surface but was so often slowed-up by miry hollows and stony ascents that it was within an hour of noon when Pontchâteau was first sighted. Windmills, leisurely at work in a light breeze, flickered in the sunshine along the crest of a low ridge to northward before the church spire appeared to mark the presence of a town. The tumbril clattered into a cobbled *place* below the church and proceeded, as if by custom, to a stone trough where the mare could quence her thirst.

Though this was not a market-day the *place* was busy with folk shopping or strolling or chatting. The sight of a respectably-dressed couple being helped out of a cabbage-cart by a big servant in a red woollen cap roused no more than a momentary interest in the passers-by. Ring's quick comprehensive survey showed him a diversity of costume, both male and female, that made the dress of himself and his companions totally inconspicuous, and the buzz of Breton voices made him feel suddenly at home and at ease. He remembered now that Redon of his boyhood stay was only a few miles north of Pontchâteau; it was not impossible that someone among this crowd had known his mother.

'Give me some money, Robert,' said Jeanne beside him. 'There are shops, and I may find you a new pair of stockings.'

Her brown eyes were merry and he grinned as he took five francs from his leather bag.

'I'll allow you ten minutes, Jeanne – not a second more,' he told her. 'I know you, when you get among the shops.'

Turfrey was lifting the pack from the cart and Ring seized the opportunity to lean under the hood and mutter a few words in his ear.

'Attend mademoiselle. I'll be back at this trough in ten minutes. No talking, remember.'

'Aye aye, sir,' Turfrey mumbled; and the response brought home to Ring the gulf that lay now between himself and his ship.

Monsieur Godinot's ancient driver had not spoken a word during the nine-mile journey and seemed disinclined to answer questions, but the sight of a silver franc opened his lips and he told Ring that there was a livery stables in the Rue Nort this side of the bridge. Jeanne and Turfrey were already vanishing into the crowd. Ring, crossing the *place* in the opposite direction, noted that none of the men he passed were young and most of them greybeards; the Emperor's latest severe conscription had taken even the teenage boys.

Hot sunshine was striking down from a clear blue sky and the shadow of the half-timbered gables of the Rue Nort was welcome. Its cobbles descended and through gaps between the buildings he caught glimpses of a river with houses rising in tiers on its green banks, and beyond them the red scar of the new road slanting up from the bridge.

Fifty paces brought him to the gates of the *écuries*, and after some hola-ing a grizzled liveryman presented himself. He was inclined to raise objections to Ring's demand for a conveyance to take three passengers to Angers – the times were bad, his best coachman taken for the army, twelve leagues was too far – but when Ring, producing his purse, showed him a gold napoleon he agreed that it might be done. A barouche, two horses; on the new road they should reach Angers before nightfall. But monsieur must understand that it would cost money –

'*Ça ne fait rien*,' said Ring. 'I travel on the Emperor's business. Government money,' he added with a wink, patting the purse in his pocket, 'and Government can pay for your best horses.'

'With taxes as they are,' said the liveryman somewhat sourly, 'Government can well afford it.'

But he lost no time in shouting for ostlers and stableboys, and Ring left him superintending the dragging-out of a four-wheeled vehicle that looked in good repair, with a high box and a hood to shelter the rear seat.

Monsieur Godinot's cabbage-cart had gone from the trough when he got back to it. In less than a minute Jeanne and

Turfrey came threading a way between the groups of gossipers.

'No stockings, Robert,' she told him as they met. 'The shops here are poor and few. But I've spent four or five francs.' She pointed to the straw bag the seaman was carrying. 'Food for our journey – did you manage to arrange a carriage?'

'Better than that, *ma soeur*. A barouche.' Ring offered his arm. 'We lie at Angers tonight.'

When they had walked to the beginning of the Rue Nort and there was no passer-by near them he spoke low-voiced over his shoulder to Turfrey behind them.

'We're going to Angers by coach, a bit short of forty miles. We shall stay at an inn – watch your tongue there.'

Turfrey acknowledged with a muted version of his deaf-and-dumb croak.

The last buckles of the harness were being fastened when they reached the stables and within five minutes they were trundling down the cobbled street behind a pair of horses which the liveryman, with the pride of a man whose countryside is famous for horse-flesh, had declared to be Léon post-horses. Turfrey having signified (literally) that he would be happy to ride on the box, he was sitting beside the veteran coachman while Ring and Jeanne occupied the rear seat. They rumbled across the little bridge over the Brivet river and turned onto the new road, where the Léon post-horses had to endure a long uphill pull before they could show their paces on the fine rolling road beyond. Unfenced, hardly rutted, with white-painted stones at the wayside to mark the *kilométres* which were the latest distance-units of France, this road seemed smooth as a billiard-table compared with the English highways Ring remembered. The barouche, he reckoned, was making a good nine knots. The sun blazed from a blue sky flecked with small white clouds and the wide countryside smiled on either hand, oddly bald to his eye because of the lack of hedges, and apparently deserted though immense fields of maize and lesser spreads of cabbages diversified the long stretches of thicket and low woodland. They overtook two crawling wagons with six-horse teams and met a farm cart, but for most of that afternoon they had the road to themselves.

Beside him Jeanne sat composedly on the leather seat, her

gaze on the changing landscape, sometimes calling his attention to an object that took her fancy – a ruined windmill, or a miniature valley with a meandering stream. The folding hood had been left down and the wind had blown off her bonnet, which was retained by its ribbons round her neck; the neatly-braided hair, the pleasure that showed in her face and eyes, gave her the look of a child enjoying its first ride in a fast carriage. One would never have thought, Ring told himself wonderingly, that little more than twelve hours ago this girl had suffered the bitterest of betrayals, had abandoned a long-established way of life for a desperate enterprise –

There his thoughts ended with an inward and somewhat wry chuckle. Nothing could seem more unlike a desperate enterprise than this idyllic ride across a peaceful countryside. *Toujours de l'audace* sounded like a mocking echo. Not much boldness had been required to hire a vehicle to Angers as any French *bourgeois* might do, when he felt himself indistinguishable from a French *bourgeois*. It was almost comforting to remember that he was a British naval officer sailing under false colours in the midst of the enemy, heading farther and farther into the country of Britain's deadliest foe.

At Nort, a little town no bigger than Pontchâteau, they paused to water the horses at a trough. Nantes was three leagues to the southward, Jeanne said; and as she spoke her face – for an instant – looked strained and old. Ring knew she was thinking of Yves de Feriet, and that despite her cheerful bearing the wound was a deep one. But an hour later, when the barouche halted again at Jeanne's request so that they could eat and drink, she had quite regained her happy composure. They had stopped on the brow of a low hill. Two or three miles ahead below a gently-falling countryside of wooded hillocks a broad river shone, its blue channels separated by islands of pale golden sand crested by green thickets. The Loire. Ring's gaze sharpened as he discerned a brown sail moving slowly downstream; Valençay was not far south of the Loire and it had occurred to him before that the river might offer a route of retreat.

'*Monsieur est servi*,' said Jeanne, and he turned to find that she had unpacked the contents of the straw bag.

She had bought bread, cheese, a knuckle of ham, and a

bottle of red *vin du pays*, together with a knife and two pottery mugs. Her other purchases, she told him as they ate, were in Antoine's pack – a larger and stronger knife, tinder-box and flint and steel.

'You're the most provident sister a man ever had,' said Ring.

'I learned to be provident when I was quite small.' Jeanne was cutting bread and meat for the two men on the box. 'When I was flying for my life across the Vendée with – with Yves, after the battle at Champtoceaux. You know of it?'

A door of Ring's memory opened suddenly. 'Champtoceaux!' he exclaimed. 'The last fight of the royalists and Chouans – Bonaparte's troops cut them to mincemeat. The royalist leader was killed. His name –' He checked himself abruptly, his gaze on Jeanne. 'His name was Bonchamps.'

'He was my father,' she said. 'It was eleven years ago. My mother had died two years before, you understand, and I was with my father, with Marthe – my old nurse – for my companion. The battle was a massacre, as you said. After it the Blues scoured the countryside slaughtering old men and women and children – all were Chouan rebels to them – and Marthe and I would have been killed but for Yves de Feriet. My father had charged him to look after us.'

'De Feriet fought in the battle?'

'He was second in command, with the cavalry. When they were broken and scattered he risked his life to come and find us. It was many days, hiding and wandering in the *bocage*, before we reached the coast. Yves was – wonderful.'

'He is not your uncle, then,' Ring said.

Jeanne stood up to hand the two mugs and the wine-bottle, now half full, to Turfrey on the box seat, signing to him to share it with the coachman. When she sat down again she answered with complete composure.

'I became his mistress. In the third year after our escape to Houat Marthe died. I was nearly sixteen.'

Ring nodded slowly. 'I understand.'

'You don't understand at all,' she told him, frowning. 'It wasn't like that – we were friends and allies as well as lovers. Yves had his bitter moods, his teasing humours, but he was brave and kind. He made me his partner in all his doings – he taught me to sail – it's hard to believe he could – could –'

With a sudden movement she turned her face away. Ring, cursing under his breath, reached a hand to cover hers where it rested on her lap.

'I'm sorry, mademoiselle,' he said gruffly.

It was a long moment before she gently withdrew her hand and turned again to look at him, with the ghost of a smile.

'Mademoiselle?' she repeated. 'I thought it was to be Jeanne and Robert between us – since we are comrades.'

'A new partnership, Jeanne,' Ring suggested, his eyes on hers.

She frowned quickly and looked away. 'All that in the past – we'll not talk of it again, if you please. Let's look to the future.' Her tone altered. 'It's a future where nothing is certain except danger. Don't you feel excited, Robert? What awaits us at the end of this road – the road to Valençay? Or on the way? It can't be all sunshine and *fêtes champêtres*.'

He laughed, answering her swift change of mood. 'For me, the road ends tonight at Angers and an inn. And we'd better be moving if we're to get there before dark.'

In the event, they reached Angers at sunset, crossing the bridge over the Maine and entering the busy streets of the old Angevin capital just as the light faded on the three towers of the cathedral. The coachman was sufficiently acquainted with the town to be able to recommend the Lion d'Or as the sort of modest inn Ring required. It proved to be an old place tucked away below the walls of the castle and looked none too clean; but when Ring, having fee'd the coachman and praised the Léon post-horses, followed Jeanne and Turfrey inside he found that the considerable *pourboire* he had given the man was well-deserved. They were the only guests, and the landlord, portly and placid, had the double merit of being both incurious and helpful. Not only did he listen sympathetically to Ring's request that Antoine (deaf and dumb, apt to get violent if other servants poked fun at him) should be allowed to sleep on a pallet in his master's room, but he also bestirred himself to assist their onward travelling. He had a horse and carriage in his own stables, he said, that would get them to Tours by noon if they were prepared to make an early start. There they must find the livery stables in the Rue Briconnet – kept by his own brother-in-law – and it was odds but they'd be in Blois before nightfall.

This was better than anything Ring had hoped for. If all went well, they would be almost within striking distance of Valençay less than forty-eight hours after leaving the coast. A week, he reminded himself, had been De Feriet's estimate for the Spaniards' secret journey. *Vive l'audace!*

They dined plainly but adequately, Turfrey with his platter and *pot* in the ingle-nook at one end of the big dining-room, and slept on beds that were at least free from vermin. Next day, at half-past seven of a dark and drizzling morning, they were away in the landlord's carriage on the road to Tours.

The carriage, fortunately a closed one, was old and smelt of rats, but it was reasonably weatherproof and the horse that pulled it, a huge animal more suited to a wagon, made light work of the hilly road. They made steady progress all that morning, passing few hamlets and travelling for much of the time through the fringes of a great forest. This time Turfrey was an inside passenger. The incessant clatter and groan of the coach kept the coachman, huddled in a multitude of capes on the box, safely out of earshot, and Ring took the opportunity to put his henchman in possession of the Valençay plan from its inception as an order from London to the hopeful picking-up of the venturers from Erdeven Point. Turfrey, sitting with folded arms in the corner of the seat opposite Ring and Jeanne, listened in silence, his craggy face intent.

''Tis a rare ticklish affair, sir,' he said when Ring invited his comments. 'You've found a way to slip us through the Frenchies, seemin'ly – that's if I can keep my mouth shut, which ain't easy – but how are we to get this Spanish king away? Will he be expectin' a rescue-party, sir?'

'I don't know, Turfrey. I know Valençay's ten leagues south of Blois where we'll be tonight, with luck. I know the name of a man who might help us when we get there. And that's all.'

Turfrey considered this for a moment. Then he chuckled. ''Tis like takin' a pheasant from squire's lawn at noonday,' he said. 'All the odds agin a man but a wunnerful feather in his cap if he brings it off.'

Jeanne, who had listened uncomprehending, leaned forward. 'I heard you speak of Erdeven, Robert,' she said. 'The ship is to wait off the point there, *n'est-ce pas?*'

'Yes, until the seventh of October. She'll stand in every midnight to watch for a signal-fire.'

'Erdeven is in my own country of the Vannetais,' she told him. 'I was born at Ploermel and I know all that countryside well – the *landes* between Châteaubriant and the coast. They used to say that the Chouans nested in the Lanvaux forests and there are still folk there who would help us – Kerzo, the miller at Callac, is one. And Callac is only a day's march from Erdeven, Robert.'

'The mill at Callac. Yes, I recall De Feriet saying –' Ring checked himself. 'Then Ploermel was your home, Jeanne?'

She nodded. 'But so long ago, Robert! I remember –'

And that began an exchange of reminiscences which beguiled them both for mile after mile of the rainswept road. Ring found it extraordinarily pleasant. Turfrey presently slumbered in his corner, and after a while Jeanne, stifling a yawn in the middle of a sentence, declared that she had slept ill at the Lion d'Or and had better make up for it now. Ring was left to stare out of the blurred window and contemplate his quite inadequate plans for what Turfrey had called 'a rare ticklish affair'.

The road here ran close to the Loire and he could see a string of timber-laden barges moving slowly on the broad river. His hazy idea of using the Loire as an escape route would have to be abandoned; it was too conspicuous a highway, with roads, bridges, towns and villages commanding it all the way to Nantes. No. Jeanne's was the only way. They'd have to recross the Loire and make their way westward across Brittany as best they could, and it would be a slow journey; no bowling along in carriages. As to Valençay and what might be done there, it was pointless to plan for that. He had no chart, no sailing-directions for those waters. When he entered them it would be dead reckoning, conning his way into blank mist as he had done on *Nonpareil*'s bowsprit off the Poulains.

Yet despite the unseen hazards Ring was content to meet them as they came. His confidence owed something to the surprising smoothness of their journey so far, and a little perhaps to the fact that his white stockings were now spotless, Jeanne having washed them; he had also shaved. But chiefly, he thought, it was due to Jeanne's presence, her companionship and support. She was the best of the good fortune that had attended this improvident expedition since its inception under a gorse-bush.

3

Their good luck stayed with them in Tours. A big town this, its cobbled streets rainswept and thinly populated. At the *écuries* in the Rue Briconnet the brother-in-law of the landlord at the Lion d'Or found them a carriage and pair to take them on to Blois and imparted some useful information in reply to cautious questioning by Ring. So they planned to look at the Château de Valençay? Ah, a fine place that – *un palais immense* – right on the edge of the forest. They said that Monsieur Talleyrand, when he was in residence, had shot a deer from the window of his chamber. The man who used to be king of Spain lived there now. To get there? If monsieur would wait a moment –

The liveryman disappeared into the shed that served as his office and returned with a soiled and crumpled paper. It was a crudely-printed schedule of dates and times headed *Compagnie des Diligences d'Anjou*, with a rudimentary map showing the main roads and the names of towns. Angers, Tours, Blois and a few other places were marked but not, Ring noted, Valençay. A tiny place, the liveryman said; nothing there but the Château. Monsieur must cross the Loire by the long bridge at Blois – here – and take the country road through the villages of Contres and Selles. Contres was four leagues from Blois, Selles four leagues beyond it and less than three from Valençay. Monsieur might keep the paper if he wished. Ring added a substantial *pourboire* to his thanks and they took the road once more.

It was nearing dusk when the muddy riverside road brought them in sight of the houses of Blois massed in tiers on their steep hillside above the river. The rain had stopped. In the last mile the carriage had overtaken a long column of infantry marching towards Blois, small men in blue coats and white breeches; the rearguard, it soon appeared, of a considerable contingent who were being billeted in Blois that night, for the streets were full of soldiers. Ring was on the lookout for the long bridge at the town's foot, and when the carriage turned opposite the bridge to climb the steep street that led from it he called to the coachman to stop at the first inn he came to. This was a big place with an ornate stone porch, every window ablaze with light and evidently full of noisy company. The landlord, a tall black-avised fellow, took in at a glance their lack of any baggage other than Turfrey's pack and declared that he could not accommodate them.

'I've a score of Hussar officers quartered on me and I'm rushed off my feet,' he added shortly. 'There's no room for you here.'

Ring, somewhat prematurely, had dismissed the carriage. He had no mind to trudge through Blois looking for another inn.

'You'll find me two rooms, and quickly,' he said peremptorily. 'I'm on Government service and I'll pay you well. This lady is my sister.'

Whether by force of the voice accustomed to command or the sight of the gold coins Ring displayed on his palm, the landlord changed his tune. Two small rooms – servants' rooms, *en effet* – might be found for monsieur and mademoiselle if they chose. The servant could perhaps sleep in the stables and eat in the kitchen. Deaf and dumb, was he? *C'est dommage* – and a man would take them to their rooms in a moment.

Small rooms they were, high under the eaves on the second floor and with no view from their windows except a prospect, four feet away, of a wet rock-face; the inn, like some others of the Blois houses, had been built into the hillside. Peering out of his window, Ring saw that six feet below him the gap was filled with solid masonry extending to the corner of the building a few yards to his right, where the roof of the stables could be discerned. He dismissed Turfrey, who had carried up their pack, to find his way to the kitchen; he could only hope that someone there would take pity on Turfrey's deficiencies. When he had made a rough toilet and Jeanne, in the candle-lit room adjoining his own, had made hers, they descended to the big dining-room.

Young men in the blue-and-silver uniform of the Hussars filled the room with loud talk and laughter, lounging around the vast fireplace where a log-fire crackled. There were no women to be seen except a stout maidservant by the door, and there was some staring and moustache-twirling as Jeanne entered on Ring's arm. He paused to bid the servant bring food and wine before steering her to the only vacant chairs in the room, which were at a side-table next to a larger table at which three men in civilian clothes sat talking over their wine. They had no sooner taken their seats than the name *Valençay* came to Ring's ears.

He had no compunction about listening. Anything he could learn about their objective, now so near, was of value. The three men had dropped their voices when the newcomers approached and for some while the conversation was inaudible, but at length one of them, a big man in a high-collared buff coat, spoke more loudly.

'I don't care what you say – it's a shame and a scandal to Blois! If he must have his *grisettes* let them be brought from somewhere else, not from our town.'

'You make too much of it, Colport,' objected one of his companions. 'The girls are whores anyway. It's trade, of a sort.'

'There's trade enough for them in Blois.' The big man drained his glass and set it down with a thump. '*Sacré!* Every time that cursed carriage crosses the bridge – and it'll be off again tomorrow morning – I consign Ferdinand to the devil.'

'Don't worry – he'll get there,' said the other. 'Two a week, *parbleu!* I wonder how many times he –'

'*Tais-toi!*' Colport muttered with a sidelong glance at Jeanne; he stood up. 'Henri will be waiting for us. *Allons.*'

The three got up and went out. Ring looked inquiringly at Jeanne, who nodded, her lips compressed.

'I heard,' she said. 'It was – our man they spoke of, I suppose?'

'Beyond a doubt. It seems they keep the scion of the Hapsburgs supplied with women.'

The approach of the maidservant with platters of food and a *pichet* of wine precluded further comment. Both of them were ready for a meal, for though the landlord's wife at the Lion d'Or had provided them with bread and meat and wine for their journey they had eaten barely half of it. As they ate they discussed tomorrow's arrangements, the noise made by the Hussar officers providing convenient cover. Before they retired

Ring, in his character as inspector of *vignobles*, would desire the landlord to provide them with a hired carriage to take them to Selles in the morning. From Selles they would find their way to Valençay on foot, arriving if possible without being seen, and try to make contact with Gril Picart, the Chouan stableman at the château. Picart, it could be presumed, would have known for some time of the intention to rescue Ferdinand and would have some plan ready. There was nothing to be done beyond this, but Jeanne's suggestion that she should buy some food as soon as the shops were open was adopted.

The meal over, Jeanne retired to her room, leaving Ring to make the arrangements for the morning with the landlord. He remained at the table for some moments, frowning at his empty plate as he considered their lack of credentials when it came to enlisting Picart's aid. When he looked up the landlord was standing beside him. The man was looking down at him with a very odd expression.

'Monsieur's servant is deaf and dumb?' he said abruptly.

'So he is.' Ring frowned annoyance. 'What is that to you?'

'Oh, nothing, monsieur – except that your servant can speak.'

'Impossible!'

'I must assure monsieur that it is so,' said the landlord; his eyes, on Ring's face, were narrowed and steady. 'My scullions were plaguing him and he became enraged. He sent one of them flying with his fist, and he spoke – very loudly. Monsieur, he spoke in English.'

Ring thought fast. '*Naturellement,*' he said impatiently. 'He has been in England. Before I engaged him he was a seaman, smuggling brandy across the Channel. The fellow must have deceived me about his dumbness.'

'Indeed?' returned the landlord drily. 'Well, monsieur, I've locked your servant in the stables. And I must ask to see your papers.'

'Devil take your impudence!' Ring's angry exclamation concealed his dismay. 'Here am I, travelling France on government business, and this is the first time an innkeeper has been insolent enough to ask to see my papers!'

'That may be,' the man said stolidly. 'It's an old law. But it's still the law that innkeepers should examine the papers of travellers, as monsieur – being of the government – must know. I demand to see monsieur's papers.'

The argument had attracted some attention from the men nearest them and the buzz of conversation had died away. A second's consideration showed Ring that he had no alternative; and in that second he saw also his only course. He stood up, glaring outraged dignity.

'Very well!' he snapped. 'You shall see them – I'll get them from my room. And when you've seen them, my man, I shall expect a very humble apology!'

He stalked out of the dining-room without looking back and went quickly up to Jeanne's room. She had not undressed except for taking off her shoes. In three rapid sentences he told her what had occurred, and the candlelight showed her expression change from dismay to a fierce determination.

'We must leave here,' she said.

'At once – with or without Turfrey. Shoes on and come into the next room.'

In his own room he opened the window wide and lowered the leather pack out by its straps; at the full stretch of his arm it touched the buttressing masonry before he let go. Jean came in after him and when he turned from bolting the door she was already climbing over the sill. He caught her arms and lowered her, then climbed out himself. They stood in the narrow space between the rock and the outer wall of the inn, not in total darkness because of the two lit windows overhead and the gleam of their reflected light from the wet rockface. Ring's feet trod on fallen rubble as he moved cautiously, with Jeanne close behind him, towards the corner of the building – to halt on the verge of a drop of some eighteen feet.

Ring cursed under his breath. He might have known there was no access to those windows from below. Opposite him across a gap too wide to leap was the roof of the stable building; the short alley below opened into the stable yard, which was faintly lit by some unseen lantern on the front of the inn. He lay down and peered over the edge. It took him a few seconds to make out the heap of earth and debris, fallen from the hillside above, that reached far up the inner wall of the alley – that should halve the drop, at any rate. He lowered Jeanne, gripping her wrists and letting her drop; heard a gasp and a scrape and a whispered '*va bien*' and at once followed, landing awkwardly on a slant of earth and stones and all but pitching headfirst onto Jeanne as she slid to the bottom of it. They stole to the open end of the alley and stood for a moment listening.

In front of them the cobbles of the stable yard sloped down to a high wall in which an archway that would admit carriages opened onto the street. The stone wall of the stables, with half-a-dozen doors in it, stretched away to their left.

They could hear noisy voices from higher up the town, and a burst of drunken singing heralded the appearance of a party of soldiers who passed the archway and went on up the street. There was no commotion in the inn so far. From nearer at hand came a quieter sound, a steady creaking and a grunting that was certainly not made by a horse. Ring listened intently for a second and then went softly along the line of doors to stop at the third he came to. It was a wooden door, thick but by no means new, and someone on the other side of it was wrenching at its planks.

'Turfrey?' he said in a low voice.

There was a brief pause. Then a very subdued voice answered. 'Aye, sir. The Frenchy as put me in here, I heard him hang the key on the wall outside. If I could ha' loosened this here board –'

'Pipe down,' Ring snapped; and over his shoulder to Jeanne, 'Get the cloaks out of the pack.'

He groped for and found the key, a massive one and rusty, hung on a nail high up on the wall. The door creaked open.

'Sir,' said Turfrey abjectly, emerging, 'I'm main sorry –'

'I said pipe down.' Ring locked the door and hung up the key. 'On cloaks.' He flung round his shoulders the cloak Jeanne handed him. 'We'll leave by the bridge –'

He stopped speaking and they stood motionless while a man passed the archway, going uphill. Ring waited while the sound of footsteps receded and then went to the archway and looked into the street. As far as he could see in the darkness there was no one in it between the inn and the riverside road fifty yards down the hill. He summoned the others and they walked out of the archway and down the street, Ring with Jeanne's arm tucked under his and Turfrey crouching beneath his cloak to conceal his height. About now, Ring was thinking, the landlord's patience would be exhausted and he would be trying the locked door of the bedroom.

They met no one. The night was a bad one for strollers, with a gusty wind blowing up the Loire and sweeping round the corner of the street. The riverside road was dark and deserted. They crossed it in silence, the wind tearing at their cloaks, and started along the bridge. No light showed in the blackness ahead. Ring felt Jeanne shiver; then her hand tightened on his arm.

'At least, Robert, we're on the road to Valençay,' she said.

The sound of the river below their feet pushing sluggishly against the stone piers was like a malicious chuckle.

VI

Toujours de l'Audace

1

Under the golden dome of the clear sky before sunrise the road lay like a taut brown ribbon stretched across the deserted countryside. With only slight undulations it ran straight as a die, rough and unfenced, through a landscape that showed neither roof nor fence and only occasionally a cleared field between the long stretches of thicket and woodland. Three figures, cloaked against the early-morning chill, moved steadily southward along the road, heading towards Valençay.

They walked at a good speed, Ring with Jeanne striding manfully beside him and Turfrey, pack on back, on his other side, and though they spoke little there was nothing in their bearing to tell that they were homeless fugitives with no resources beyond the dwindling store of money in Ring's pocket. All three of them were of that sanguine temperament for which a night's sleep, breakfast, and the prospect of a fine day can turn a hopeless future into a field of opportunity.

That they had slept well and warmly was due to Turfrey. The bridge over the Loire and the cluster of dark buildings at its outward end were left behind, the lights of Blois had dwindled and vanished, and they had made a good four miles along the straight rain-puddled road before Ring was satisfied that they were beyond the reach of a possible pursuit. Shelter and sleep seemed unattainable, until Turfrey's countryman's nose had detected a barn half-full of dry hay behind some trees twenty paces from the lane. They had lain down wrapped in their cloaks on this warm and scented bed, rousing at dawn to breakfast on the scanty remains of yesterday's lunch and take the road again in the growing light. Over breakfast Ring and

Jeanne had discussed their situation and Ring had reported the gist of it to Turfrey, whose fateful slip at the inn had been punished (his commanding officer having no use for recrimination) by the stoppage of his rum ration until further notice; a sentence pronounced and accepted without a smile • on either side.

An absconding customer without papers, with a deaf-and-dumb servant who spoke English, was certainly matter for a report to the *préfecture* and subsequent inquiry and search, but not (Ring thought) warrant for an immediate hue-and-cry. No one had seen them leave Blois, no one could guess what route they had taken. Enlistment of the Hussars to scour the roads for them was unlikely – the affair was too slight for that. So they would press on towards Valençay, that being as good a direction as any, and hope to find at Contres – now little more than two leagues distant – some sort of wheeled vehicle to carry them on their way. To Jeanne's proposal that they should leave the road and move in cover beside it Ring returned a decided negative; only on the road could they move fast, and speed was more than ever indispensable to them now. He knew (though he would not admit it, either to his companions or to himself) that any hope they might have had of achieving their purpose was fast dwindling, but he was not going to give up.

The sun rose over wooded hills on their left as they trudged on. Ring ordered Turfrey to keep a lookout astern. It was mere prudence not to be seen if they could avoid it, and there were always bushes or trees at the wayside for them to dodge into at need. He was somewhat surprised that they had so far had the road to themselves; French peasants began work early and he would have expected to meet market-wagons making for Blois and labourers in field or forest using the road. Jeanne reminded him that it was Sunday, when no one in farm or village worked or travelled. As she was speaking, the road was entering an arm of the large forest that spread to westward, and they were hardly beneath the barred shadows of the trees when Turfrey spoke.

'Carriage comin' up astern, sir.'

Turning, Ring saw it half-a-mile away on the straight ribbon of road, a mere speck but approaching at good speed. His decision was instantly made: whoever this early traveller was, he should take them on board. He hurried his companions on, keeping close in to the roadside, to where a screen of alder overhung the bracken-filled ditch and they could crouch in its cover, peering through the yellow leaves. The carriage came on, two horses at a spanking trot, a fat coachman on the box wearing a purple coat and an old-fashioned *tricorne*. It could only have come from Blois, starting early. A smart turnout, smart enough for the Château de Valençay –

Into Ring's mind flashed phrases he had overheard at the inn last night: *that cursed carriage ... it'll be off again tomorrow morning*. This was King Ferdinand's weekly consignment of women.

'Off pack!' he snapped at Turfrey. 'Get out the two knives. Stand by here until I give the word, then catch the horses' heads. Any experience of horses?'

'Brung up as a stable-lad, sir.'

The carriage was entering the shadows of the wood. Ring handed the smaller of the two knives bought at Pontchâteau to Jeanne, who was staring at him wide-eyed. He found time for a reassuring grin.

'We need this carriage. When I shout, run to the door and open it. Threaten whoever's inside with the knife if they move.'

The rumble of wheels was very close and before she could reply he had sprung out into the middle of the road. In his left hand, behind his back, he grasped the larger knife, a woodsman's tool with a seven-inch blade and a sharp point. His right hand, aloft at full stretch, arrested the carriage, which reined to a halt amid a trampling of hooves and a stream of oaths from the fat coachman.

'*Pardon, mon ami*,' Ring shouted cheerily, 'but I travel to the Château at Valençay on urgent business. You can take me there, if you will.'

Two heads in frilly bonnets thrust themselves out of the carriage window. The coachman scowled doubtfully at the man in the road; there was enough of the gentleman about Ring to make him hesitate.

'And who's your business with at the Château, monsieur?' he demanded.

'With a man named Gril Picart.'

The coachman snorted. 'Then you'd best ask for the Widow

Picart. Picart broke his neck a fortnight ago when the new stallion threw him.'

The shock of this unlucky news held Ring silent for a breathing-space. The coachman had time to make up his mind.

'What's more,' he said offensively, 'you can get out of my way. I don't give lifts to vagabonds.' He gathered his reins. 'Stand clear!'

This was what Ring had anticipated. A glance showed him the road still deserted as far as he could see and with a shout of 'Away boarders!' he leaped to the box-seat, knife displayed. Too late the coachman reached for the whip in its socket beside him. A hand gripped his collar and the glittering knife-point pressed against his ribs.

'Hold hard or I'll cut your liver out,' Ring snarled with all the ferocity he could command.

The horses neighed and trampled but Turfrey had them fast. A duet of squeals, suddenly cut short, sounded from the body of the coach. He had taken his prize – but what was he to do with the prisoners?

'*Ayez p-p-pitie, monsieur!*' faltered the coachman; his fat face had turned a purplish white and he was shaking like a jelly. 'I have s-seven children –'

'Answer my questions or they'll be fatherless.' The knife-point pressed harder. 'Does Madame Picart – Picart's widow – live in the Château?'

'N-no, monsieur – in the village – Valençay.'

'Where is her house? Quickly, if you wish to live.'

The coachman's words tumbled over each other but the directions were clear enough. There was a long avenue leading to the gates of the Château, a lane running to the right outside the gates; monsieur would come at once to the few houses of the village and Madame Picart's was the last house on the left, with a large stable beside it. Ring would have liked to ask more questions but he dared not spend time. At any moment, Sunday or not, a vehicle or horseman might approach along the sunlit road. He jabbed the knife-point urgently.

'Get down – and no tricks!'

He followed the coachman as the man climbed shakily down to the road. Jeanne, her round face fiercely contorted, was

standing at the open door of the coach with her small knife
pointing threateningly at the occupants. Ring winked at her
and waved her back a pace.

'Outside with you, mesdemoiselles!' he ordered sharply. 'Do
exactly as you're told and no harm shall come to you.'

Two buxom girls emerged, their pretty painted faces
showing expressions between fright and excitement. Ring, his
knife held against the coachman's back, rapped orders. Jeanne
to the horses' heads; Turfrey to follow him with the girls; and
to the coachman, 'March!' Thrusting the unhappy man in
front of him, he crossed the ditch and began to force a way into
the forest.

Force was necessary, for a yard or two inside the trees the
bracken, already turning gold, grew shoulder-high, and
beneath it was a yielding network of brambles. For all his
urging progress was slow. The coachman whimpered as the
thorns tore at his plump legs, the two girls emitted continuous
shrieks of protest. Louder squeals, just after he had laboriously
pushed his prisoner through a high thicket of arching
brambles, made Ring turn. He saw one of the girls rising from
the bracken where she had fallen while Turfrey, on the other
side of the thicket, was lifting the other girl in his arms
preparatory to tossing her over. Judging by the broad grin on
his face Turfrey was enjoying himself.

Time was flying and Ring went only a dozen yards farther,
halting where a patch of moss made an island amid the
thickets. Turfrey's charges were both in tears by now, their
gaudy dresses in rags; they sank down moaning beside the
coachman, who had collapsed exhausted on the moss. Ring
himself was breathing hard and sweating mightily, for the
windless morning was increasingly warm as the sun rose
higher. He was hurriedly seeking some means short of violence
for delaying his victims' escape from the forest when Turfrey
presented him with the simple solution.

'So please ye, sir – off wi' their shoes?'

'Well thought of, Turfrey. Make it so.'

They removed the shoes from three pairs of feet without the
least resistance from their owners and hurled them far into the
thickets. Then, pausing only to snatch the *tricorne* from the
coachman's head, Ring led the painful way back to the road as

fast as he could go. It was a relief to see Jeanne still standing patiently at the horses' heads, the horses quiet, the road as deserted as ever. The girl was looking anxious.

'You've not killed them, Robert?' she asked as he got across the ditch.

'*Bon Dieu!*' Ring was amused. 'They're as unharmed as I am, my dear.' His white stockings, he saw, were badly torn and streaked with blood. 'Please to get in, Mademoiselle Bague, and I'll drive you to Valençay. Turfrey, inside with mademoiselle – and rig the curtains over those windows.'

He stowed the knives in the pack and handed it to Jeanne, then climbed to the box and settled the coachman's *tricorne*, which was of purple felt edged with silver braid, on his head; it was a tight fit but so it should be. Jeanne waited until he had gathered the reins and then got in. It was some years since he had handled the ribbons but the horses, a well-trained and docile pair, responded to his signals. The carriage, with a lurch and a jolt, trundled off.

Ring urged his horses to their former fast trot. Seven or possibly eight knots, he told himself, and the narrow country road good of its kind – that should bring them to Contres in less than an hour. Then twelve miles to Selles and another eight to Valençay. Barring mischance, they'd be there before noon. Sounds from inside the carriage indicated that Jeanne and Turfrey were attempting conversation, and he heard Jeanne laugh. Incontinently his spirits rose, and he wondered at himself. No forlorn hope could be more forlorn than this mad drive in a stolen carriage, through an enemy's country, towards an enemy stronghold, their one hope of entering the stronghold gone, the hue-and-cry certain to be out for them before the end of the day. Their armament consisted of two knives and their only assets were a little money and – *l'audace*. Boldness had won the carriage – it was, he realised, that swift little action that had exhilarated him – and boldness alone could carry them any farther. He felt, as he always did, that the momentum must be kept up. At Valençay, if the least chance offered, it must be *toujours de l'audace*.

A speck on the road ahead developed into a horse with two riders, an elderly couple with the woman riding pillion. Ring touched a careless finger to his hat as they met and drove on without looking round. The sun of late summer blazed with more than autumnal brilliance from a sky of clear pale blue, the wide deserted landscape smiled on either hand, and somewhere ahead a church bell pealed, its clangour mellowed to music by distance. It was very difficult in this atmosphere of Sabbath peace to remember that all three of them carried their lives in their hands.

Precisely between the edges of the road as it topped a rise far ahead rose a church spire. Ring reached behind him to tap on the carriage roof and called a warning that they were approaching Contres. When they came to it, Contres proved to be a cobbled street of houses with the church as its centre. Except for two cats and one small girl carrying a baby, the street was empty; everyone was at Mass. The carriage clattered through and out on the road to Selles, to halt five miles farther on where the road crossed a ford to water the horses. Another steeple presented itself ahead on the straight road and they rolled into Selles, where the folk in their best finery were coming out of church and Ring had to walk his horses, returning a wave and a mumbled response to two men who called after the carriage.

Then Selles was left behind, and they rattled in a cloud of reddish dust along a rougher road. For mile after mile the undulating country of woods and thickets and swampy meres slid behind them, with only an occasional prairie-like field. Soon, ahead and to the right, the green-gold carpet of an extensive forest spread itself. They met no one, and there was no sign that they were in the near vicinity of '*un palais immense*'. This château of Valençay, Ring reflected, must be the remotest in France; no doubt that was why the Emperor had selected it for the detention of the King of Spain. He took the whip from its socket and tickled the horses to a faster pace.

The tall ranked trees of an avenue rose on the horizon in front and when its welcome shade received the carriage he drove more slowly. For half-a-mile the avenue ran dead straight, aimed at the huge wrought-iron gates in a long wall at its end, and as the gates came nearer Ring braced himself, ready to halt, turn, and run for it. Two-and-a-half days had passed since the seizure of the Spanish agents on the coast at La Turballe. If the alarm had been given, if a messenger had arrived from Nantes, the Château might be on the alert, improbable though an attempt to free Frederick would appear when the rescue-party had been captured. And here he was driving his purloined carriage up to the gates! It was *l'audace* carried to an extreme.

But the gates were unguarded and the stone lodge to the left of them showed no sign of life. The only people in sight outside the wall were a lad and a girl in the long grass under the trees, who interrupted their courting to wave at the carriage. Ring nodded curtly at them and swung the carriage to the right just short of the gates, where a broad lane ran below the wall. As he did so he had his first glimpse of the Château through the iron scroll-work of the gates. Beyond a level garden as big as a cricket-field dotted with statuary and stone-rimmed pools sprawled a vast square building three stories high, with ugly bulbous domes at each corner. One or two human figures, gardeners perhaps, moved among the flower-beds. Then he was past and the houses of the village were close ahead.

Ring took a deep breath. The carriage and its usual coachman must be known to every person in this tiny hamlet, the hat he was wearing (he snatched it off and substituted his own) recognisable as the coachman's personal property. And how the devil was he to explain himself when he was challenged, as he must be? *L'audace* couldn't help him here. The carriage entered the little street of neat cottages.

There was not a soul to be seen. Ring could hardly credit this good fortune, until a savoury smell came to his nostrils – it was the hour of *déjeuner*. Beyond the last house he could see a somewhat larger dwelling on the left of the lane, with a long open barn or stable next to it; the Picarts' house, if the coachman could be trusted. Another hundred yards –

'*Holà, cocher!*' A stocky man, shirt-sleeved, had hailed him from the doorway of the last cottage. 'Where's Gruvel?'

Ring reined-in his horses. He had no alternative but to reply and his story had better be a good one.

'In Blois,' he said. 'He was taken ill.'

'*Tiens*! Seriously?'

'No – stomach trouble. But he couldn't drive so they put me on the box instead.'

'Ah. Haven't seen you before. Unloaded your goods, have you?' added the man with a grin and a wink.

Ring grinned back. 'I have. I was told to find a Madame Picart here.'

'*Bien sûr!* It's where they keep that carriage – down there on the left. The old girl will damn your soul to hell but don't mind her.'

Ring nodded thanks and drove slowly on, swallowing hard as he did so. He felt like a man walking a tightrope in the dark with unseen hands propping him up whenever he missed his footing. Gruvel (by now the coachman must have crawled out of the forest) would doubtless have had the gates opened and driven up to the Château. That the lodgekeeper hadn't glaned from his window and seen the carriage turn towards the village, that Picart's stables should be where the carriage was normally housed – this was pure luck. Fortune was certainly with them once more. But what had the fellow meant by the old girl damning his soul?

He turned the horses in through the gateless entrance of a large unpaved courtyard partly shaded by an ancient elm. The inner side was filled by the long open barn, with wooden-doored loose-boxes at its farther end, which backed against the high wall of the Château. To the left of the barn was a neat stone cottage with a small fenced garden in front of it. Ring drew up close to the wall in the narrow space between cottage and barn. There was an iron ring on the wall with a coil of line hung on it, and he jumped down to secure the horses to this before running back to open the carriage door a few inches.

'We're at Valençay,' he said rapidly. 'Picart's house. Stay where you are while I reconnoitre.'

Jeanne's voice answered from the dark interior. 'But Picart is dead – the coachman said so. What can you do?'

'I can find Madame Picart. There's a chance she –'

'I am Madame Picart,' said a harsh voice behind Ring.

He swung round. Confronting him was a short, very broad woman dressed entirely in black except for the lace bonnet perched on a tight bun of coarse black hair. Two exceedingly sharp black eyes scrutinised Ring's face briefly. Then, before he could open his mouth, she brushed past him and pulled the carriage door wide open. For perhaps five seconds she stood motionless, staring inside.

Ring found his voice. 'Madame,' he began.

But she had turned and was marching past him in the direction of the cottage.

'You will come into my house,' she threw over her shoulder. 'All three of you.'

2

No fire burned in the fireplace of the low-beamed kitchen and its coolness was welcome after the heat of the journey. They sat round a scrubbed wooden table as Madame Picart's imperative gesture required; Jeanne composed but anxious, Turfrey puzzled and watching his commanding officer, Ring hiding indecision behind an impassive countenance. Madame Picart stood with folded arms looking down at them. She had a large nose, and the incipient moustache beneath it added to the masculinity of her angular face.

'You will tell me who you are and what you want here,' she said uncompromisingly.

Ring, quite at a loss, played for time. 'Naturally, madame,' he assured her. 'But first allow us to offer our sympathy. We were concerned to hear of your husband's death –'

'It was the wages of sin,' she said unexpectedly. 'Tophet is ordained of old for such as he. You may spare your sympathy.' Her stern expression had not changed. 'Who told you of it?'

'Gruvel the coachman.'

She snorted. 'That pimp! He and Gril have been panders to that son of Belial in the Château for the last three years. Sold themselves to the devil. What have you done with Gruvel?'

Ring hesitated only for a moment. This woman had them in her power. He baulked at the idea of silencing her by force. Moreover, the few words she had spoken hinted that to tell her the truth might not be a bad course. He took the plunge and in a few quick sentences told how they had captured the coach and dealt with its driver and passengers. Madame Picart's face looked as if it never smiled, but her rigid severity relaxed a little.

'Gruvel got less than his deserts,' she pronounced judicially. 'Gril Picart has paid in full. Yet, monsieur –' it was the first time she had called him that – 'I'd have you know that these poor sinners were not the source of evil. That's in the Château yonder, with his whores and his wine-bibbing.' Her harsh voice rose a tone. 'A time will come when the dogs shall fatten on his blood as they did on the blood of Jezebel wife of Ahab! God will not look favourably on Valençay while he's here.'

'You speak of Ferdinand, king of Spain, I think,' Ring said slowly.

'I do,' she snapped. 'And the sooner he's back in his kingdom the better, say I.'

Ring glanced across the table at Jeanne. Her slight nod seemed to show that she knew what was in his mind and approved it.

'Madame Picart,' he said, regarding her steadily, 'I am going to place our lives in your hands. Our names don't matter, but we are here to try and get the king secretly away from Valençay. If –'

'You are not Spanish,' she interrupted with a frown.

He took that up quickly. 'Your husband told you Spaniards might be coming here?'

'Gril told me nothing, monsieur.' Her sharp black eyes dwelt a moment on Turfrey. 'That man is neither Spanish nor French.'

'My servant is an Englishman, madame, and so am I.'

'Ah. And mademoiselle?'

Jeanne answered. 'I am Breton, of the Vannetais, madame.'

'I come from Niort, myself,' said Madame Picart; she marched across to a tall cupboard in the wall. 'When did you last eat?' she demanded with her back to them.

'At daybreak, madame,' Jeanne told her.

'You're not starving, then. As far as I can see, you've no hope at all of getting the Spanish king away.' As she spoke she banged a plate of maize-cakes down on the table. 'If you're thinking to reach the sea it's fifty leagues from here.' She added a dish of butter and three knives. 'You had to steal a carriage to get here and Gruvel will send the Law to chase you.' A bottle of red wine and three small thick tumblers joined the rest. 'But I'll help you if I can. What do you want to know?'

'*Grand merci, madame,*' Ring said. 'But what if someone from the village were to find us here? It would be as bad for you as for us.'

'No one from the village will come here,' returned Madame Picart with finality. 'They are Catholics. I follow Jean Calvin. I am a *paria* – they tell their children I'm a witch.' She sat down near the table and jabbed a finger at him. '*Mangez, mangez.* Talk while you eat.'

The maize-cakes were very hard but good, and the wine better. The three of them fell to work and Ring, between mouthfuls, put questions which Madame Picart answered with admirable conciseness. The results were not encouraging. She had never been in the Château and could only tell what she had learned from her husband. There were about fifty people in the Château including the cooks and servants. The King of Spain and his small entourage of valets and attendants inhabited the west wing – she had no idea where Ferdinand's chamber was situated – and here also lived a priest and Monsieur de Beauregard who (Ring gathered) was a kind of major-domo for the establishment. The east wing housed the guard, a dozen hussars under a lieutenant, and their horses were stabled within the Château wall. No, they never mounted a guard round the place – why should they? Where could the young man go if he chose to run away? Not that he would want to run away from the good food and wine and the wenches they brought in for him, added Madame Picart with a *pouf*! of disgust. As for getting into the Château to speak to the King, that was *tout-à-fait impossible*. So was getting a message to him; she could not go in herself and there was no one who could be trusted for such a thing.

'Does the King never come outside the walls?' Ring asked.

'Sometimes. Perhaps once in two weeks.' She darted a penetrating glance at him. 'If you're thinking of playing the *voleur de grand chemin* again you can give up that idea. Two hussars always ride behind his carriage.'

And in any case, he reflected, they couldn't wait until Ferdinand took his next drive. In fact, they couldn't afford to wait at all. He asked if she knew how the King spent the hours of daylight. It was said that he never rose before midday, she told him, and then he was always bad-tempered after last night's drinking. On a fine day he might walk about in the gardens, even take his *p'tit déjeuner* outside if it was warm enough – she herself had seen him doing that.

'In the gardens?' Ring demanded quickly. 'Those one can see through the gates?'

Madam Picart stared at him in silence for a moment. 'It is possible,' she said as if to herself. 'It's just possible that he would come there on a hot day like this. No, monsieur,' she went on more quickly. 'On the other side, the south side. You must understand that the land falls away steeply there to a small valley. There are terraces and flowers and little ponds. The young man was sitting there when I saw him. Two months ago it was, in July.'

'What is he like?' Jeanne put in unexpectedly.

'A shrimp of a man, mademoiselle. Thin, sallow – nothing like a king. I'd been been gathering firewood – the forest comes almost to the garden fence on the west side – and from the corner one can see the terraces. I went to look and there he was, on the terrace above what they call the Duchess's Garden.'

Ring thought fast. They had reached their objective with at most only a few hours in hand. What now presented itself was the thinnest of chances, a length of spun-yarn dangled before a drowning man, but he had to grasp it if he could. If he couldn't there would be no other opportunity, for they must take to their heels like a trio of hunted foxes, escaping on foot into the forest that offered its refuge so conveniently. Unless –

'Madame,' he said abruptly, 'the road here runs westward. Where does it lead?'

'Through the forest to Montrésor,' she answered, watching him narrowly. 'A little road but good for carriages. Five leagues to Montrésor.'

'And beyond Montrésor?'

'To Loches and Chinon. Then to Saumur on the Loire, nearly thirty leagues from here.' She rubbed her chin meditatively, her eyes still fixed on his face. 'You'd not get that far. The hussars, as I've told you, have horses. A man in a stolen carriage,' she added slowly, 'might leave it and take to the forest.'

Ring caught the sparkle of excitement under the heavy black brows and smiled. 'So he might, madame. And he would give thanks.' He rose to his feet. 'And now I ask only that you tell us how to gain the forest outside the fence –'

'Finish your wine,' Madame Picart told Turfrey, who gaped uncomprehendingly and then drained his glass. 'With or without,' she added to Ring, getting up, 'you'll want to go fast when you leave here. I'll see to the horses. Come.'

She waved aside Ring's attempted thanks with a hand like a ploughman's and they followed her out into the hot sunshine. Valençay seemed asleep in the windless noon of a St Martin's Summer, the lane deserted, the other houses of the village hidden by the leafy branches of the elms. Madam Picart led them round the back of the carriage, casting a critical eye over the horses as she passed between them and the end of the barn, and halted a few paces along the narrow gap between the back of the barn and the lofty stone wall. A wooden door green with age was set in an archway in the wall.

'Here is your way,' she said briefly.

Ring told Turfrey to fetch the pack from the carriage and turned a frowning face to Madame Picart.

'Madame,' he said, 'we may achieve something or nothing. In either case you will be accused of helping us.'

For the first time she smiled, grimly. 'You think I might join the company of martyrs? Well, monsieur –' she pointed – 'there is my house. The door is the only one and the key is on the outside. The windows are too small for me to get out of. Before you leave – that is if you find yourself able to leave – turn the key, if you will. You will have forced me to show you this door and then locked me in. *C'est tout.*'

She turned away without another word, brushing past Turfrey returning with the pack. Ring pulled back the heavy bolt and pushed the door open, pausing before he followed the others through the doorway to glance after Madame Picart. She was standing by the horses with her back to him, her strong brown fingers busy unbuckling the harness. She didn't look round.

On the other side of the doorway a grassy bank, short and steep, led up to level ground where the three halted to get their bearings. They were standing in a corner formed by the high wall which presumably enclosed the grounds of the Château and a stout wooden fence seven feet high that stretched ahead on their left. On the right was the fringe of the forest, a partly cleared area of bushes and sparse trees that grew more densely a hundred paces in to become what looked like impenetrable woodland.

Through a crack in the closely-set planking of the fence Ring could see the formal garden, sunlit and apparently deserted, with its low box hedges and flower-beds spreading away to the long western façade of the Château. The pale-brown flank of a deer, glimpsed as it disappeared into the forest thickets, gave the reason for the tall fence. He signed to Jeanne and Turfrey to bring their heads close to his and spoke low-voiced, at first in French.

'I want to find a place where we can see the terraces on the south. There's a chance that we might see the King.'

'And if we do?' demanded Jeanne.

'We may be able to attract his attention, perhaps speak to him.'

Her brown eyes regarded him steadily. 'It's a very small chance, Robert. And you realise we've no time to do anything, even if we can approach him without being seen.'

'It's a very small chance, Jeanne,' Ring agreed gravely, 'but it's our last chance. More likely than not it will come to nothing – and then we must save ourselves if we can. But if Fortune should offer the least hint of opportunity I intend to jump at it.' He smiled down at her. 'Are you with me?'

'Of course.' She reached out a hand impulsively. 'We are comrades, are we not?'

Ring caught her hand and pressed it briefly. Then he told Turfrey what he proposed. The seaman's only reaction was to cast a glance from the ground ahead of them to the clear blue sky overhead.

'Sun's on this side the fence,' he remarked. 'By y'r leave, sir, we'd best move along well clear of it. A man in them gardens could see us passin' the cracks.'

Ring nodded; the ex-poacher was in his element here. 'Lead on, then.'

Turfrey's course skirted the outlying gorse-clumps and bushes between fence and forest, keeping just so far away from the fence that it screened them from the upper windows of the Château. The warm still air of early afternoon held the cooing of wood-pigeons in the forest boughs and occasional sounds from beyond the fence – a distant and transient hum of voices, a sudden quacking of ducks, the whinny of a horse. Five minutes of fast walking across level ground brought them to the rim of a shallow valley, wild and uninhabited, beyond whose meandering stream trees and thickets at a lower level stretched far away into the haze.

It could be seen now that the Château buildings formed a hollow square fronting the steep descent to the valley. The fence they had been following turned sharply to the left on the brow of the hill, running slightly downward to end against the buttressing wall of the lowest of three terraces. Ring left Turfrey and Jeanne at this corner, well screened except from the valley below, and went forward to reconnoitre.

From the base of the fence the ground fell away steeply in stony turf thatched with brambles. Above on his left the bulbous dome at the end of the west wing loomed against the sky. The buttressing wall rose from the slope to support a low balustrade of mossy stone, and when he reached it he found it easy to raise himself cautiously and look over the balustrade. The terrace that confronted him looked as if it was unused; it was certainly untended, with a few weed-grown flower-beds dotting stone slabs sprouting grass from their cracks. Crumbling stone steps led up from it to the next terrace. All he could see of this was that it lay below the long balustrade of the uppermost terrace, which was at the level of the wide courtyard between the two wings of the Château. Two enormous stone urns flanked the opening of a wide stairway descending to the middle terrace.

Ring crouched below the rank of dwarfish stone pillars to make a rapid assessment of the situation. Generations of gardeners had thrown the refuse of their craft over the bottom balustrade and there was now a flowery bank running along below it at the top of the hillside; from many places it was easy to step over, and there was nothing to hinder him from walking straight up into the Château courtyard – except that this would be putting his head into the lion's mouth. He had only to be seen and the slender thread of their sole chance was broken. He scrambled back to the others and gave them a whispered report.

'Then we must wait,' Jeanne murmured, 'and hope.'

'And listen,' Ring added. 'We'll stop talking now.'

They settled themselves on the grass at the foot of the fence above the slope of the hillside. From here the balustrade of the lowest terrace could be seen but nothing of the others. Turfrey had taken off his pack and sat with his back against it, Jeanne had clasped her hands round knees drawn up under her voluminous skirt and was gazing out over the sunlit valley. They might, thought Ring, have been a trio of Sunday ramblers resting from their stroll instead of a band of desperadoes in imminent danger of capture. And 'imminent' was no empty word. The certainty of discovery loomed very near now; a few hours, perhaps only minutes, and the inhabitants of this sleepy Château would be out after them like a swarm of angry bees.

Ring visualised Gruvel emerging at the roadside to hail a passing horseman with his news, the man he had spoken to in the village reporting the tale of the strange coachman to the lodgekeeper. At this very moment, if the resultant alarm had been given, the lieutenant of hussars and his men might be questioning Madame Picart, finding the unbolted door, advancing along the forest fringe. To sit here inactive waiting for a sign that might never be given, while inevitable doom crept every moment nearer, was worse than awaiting the first broadside from an enemy ship.

Insects flitted and hummed among the flowers on the hill-slope. In the far distance a cow lowed once or twice and then was silent. Half-an-hour passed without a sound from the direction of the Château terraces.

3

Turfrey was the first to alert the party. He sat up suddenly, raising a significant finger and nodding at Ring. At first they heard only the faint murmur of men's voices, barely audible. Then the voices grew louder and one of them, a high imperious voice, seemed to produce an echo, from which Ring deduced that the speakers were in the courtyard between the wings of the Château. He moved along the descending base of the fence to a place where the narrow spaces between the planking, and a fortunate knot-hole, enabled him to get a constricted and imperfect view of the courtyard balustrade and the terraces below it.

The upper halves of three men came into sight almost at once, walking slowly behind the balustrade. As they passed the wide opening that gave onto the double stairway he saw them at full length: a tall man in soutane and priest's hat, a stouter man of equal height in a purple coat, and a short slim figure dressed in black coat and close-fitting pantaloons with a white frill to his shirt. They were too far from his viewpoint for features to be distinguished or conversation overheard, but Ring thought it very probably that the small man in black was King Ferdinand the Seventh of Spain.

The three strolled the length of the balustrade and turned to walk slowly back again. Ring watched them with hope surging up in him. Two minutes' conversation with the King, if he could somehow contrive it without being discovered, might bring his hastily-made plan to fruition. It was not (in Ring's estimation) a good plan, because he had to rely on someone other than himself, but it was the best he could devise. The initial move would have to be made by the King himself. With luck, Ring hoped to get the carriage away and some miles along the Montrésor road, where in the flanking forests he could find a place to conceal it until the following day. He would return after dark below the terraces and meet the King there, escorting him back to the carriage; but Ferdinand would have to find the means of getting out of the Château by night and down to the lower terrace. It should not be impossible if he had resolution enough. And then –

A voice, loud and impatient, made him return his attention to his peep-holes. The man in black (it must surely be the King) had halted with the others at the head of the steps, and was gesturing to someone out of sight in the courtyard. One after the other three men in purple livery appeared above the steps, each carrying a burden and each making a kind of cringe as he passed the King, and began to descend to the middle terrace. One carried a small table, another a chair, and the third a tray covered with a white cloth. They started to set these out in the centre of the terrace but hastily moved them close to the outer balustrade at a shrill order from above. The cloth was spread on the table; the tray, holding a bottle of wine and a glass, was placed on the cloth. One of the men laid a folded newspaper on the table and they all went to the foot of the steps. Ferdinand was descending the stairway, slowly and with a certain wavering of his thin legs that made Ring wonder whether he had already taken a sufficiency of wine. He passed the bowing servants without a glance and sauntered over to the table.

Ring waited no longer. The two men with whom the King had been talking had resumed their promenade beside the upper balustrade, in full view of the man at the table, but a chance might offer and he must be in position ready to take it. He scrambled back to the others and whispered his news and his instructions. Turfrey was to keep watch on their escape route, Jeanne to come with him. He could hear the girl's fast excited breathing as, crouching like himself, she followed him down to the foot of the buttressing wall below the bottom terrace. Here they could see nothing of what was above them, but Ring had noted a place a few yards farther along where a bush of lavender, self-setting in the bank of garden refuse, had grown so high as to screen the pillars of the balustrade. They scrambled up side by side until they could peer upward through the sweet-scented twigs.

The King's head and shoulders were in view as he sat at his table behind the balustrade above. Despite the unseasonable heat of the sun he was hatless, his black hair long and elaborately curled. He threw back his head to drain his glass of wine and they saw a thin sallow face, effeminate for all its big nose and protruding lower lip. Above and beyond him the courtyard balustrade could be seen, with the priest and his companion still at their to-and-fro strolling.

Ring measured the distance with his eye: a good hundred and fifty feet between himself and that table – he'd have to raise his voice for that and it was likely to reach the ears of the men above. Ferdinand would have to come down to him. He watched the promenaders carefully. So far as he could tell at this distance they were closely engaged in talk and paid no attention to their royal charge. Suppose he attracted the King's attention with a flung stone and then showed himself. It was at least an even chance that Ferdinand would call out to demand what he was doing there and so alert the men on the upper terrace, but it looked as though he'd have to take that chance.

'Robert.' Jeanne, close beside him, had her mouth almost against his ear. 'Perhaps he would come down – for me.'

He turned his head to look at her. A little smile trembled on her lips and her eyes were dancing; she had been quick to perceive his problem. Ring glanced up at the courtyard balustrade and saw that the walkers were moving so far back that only the tops of their heads showed. It was now or never. He looked at Jeanne again and nodded. With his help she pulled herself up until she was standing beside the lavender bush, the balustrade waist-high against her. With one hand on the stonework, she undid the buttons of her bodice with the other, glancing down at him as she did so.

That picture of her stayed with Ring for a long time: the sunlight glinting on the braided coils of her hair, the mingling of daring and shyness in the brown eyes that met his, the smooth roundness of the breasts that emerged from the loosened bodice. With something of a wrench he brought his attention back to the man at the table above him. Ferdinand had taken up the newspaper and was unfolding it with unsteady fingers. It slipped from his grasp and with a muttered oath he bent to pick it up. As he straightened himself his downward glance fell on Jeanne and he stayed half-stopped and open-mouthed, staring at her. Jeanne laid a finger against her lips and beckoned, smiling seductively. Ferdinand let the newspaper fall and stood up.

Ring, watching from behind his lavender screen, saw the King turn to look back towards the courtyard and for a moment thought he was about to call to his keepers. But Jeanne had not misjudged him; he was looking to see that he was unobserved. An ugly grin on his sallow face, his eyes on Jeanne and her charms, he started down the crumbling steps. He was halfway down them when his foot struck a fragment of rubble. He staggered, lost balance, and pitched forward to land with a thud on the stone slabs of the terrace and lie face downwards, motionless.

Jeanne's involuntary exclamation as Ferdinand slipped appeared to have attracted no attention from the men in the courtyard. She shrank back into cover at Ring's urgent gesture and he swung himself over the balustrade. Three paces took him out of sight of the courtyard, below the rise of the middle terrace, and he ran to kneel beside the King. A little blood was oozing from a contusion on the back of his skull and he was quite unconscious. Ring rolled him over and slid a hand inside the frilled shirt; at least he was not dead, and a quick examination showed that there was no fracture of arm or leg. But it might be long before he recovered his senses. The plan of arranging a rendezvous had to be replaced by a new one. He called to Jeanne as loudly as he dared.

'Bring Turfrey, quick as you can.'

He heard the rustle and scrape as she went. With his hands under the fallen man's armpits he dragged him across the stone slabs until he was just within the screen afforded by the terrace wall. A cautious survey showed no one in sight above – presumably they had moved farther back in the courtyard. From behind the balustrade came a mutter indicating that Turfrey had arrived.

'Keep down,' Ring told him in a hoarse whisper. 'Stand by to take him.'

It was done quickly. Five seconds sufficed to get the limp body to the balustrade and heave it over into Turfrey's waiting arms. Only when he himself was over and crouching in cover did Ring look up again at the courtyard, and his heart gave an unpleasant bump when he saw two figures standing motionless at the upper balustrade. Then they moved, walking slowly along as before. Perhaps they had seen the vacant table; if so, they would at first assume that Ferdinand had gone down to the lower terrace, out of sight. When he had not returned after ten or fifteen minutes they would come down to investigate. He signed to Jeanne to go in front, Turfrey to take Ferdinand's shoulders, lifted the legs himself. Fortunately they had no heavy weight to carry – not more than nine stone, Ring thought – but even so it was a relief to gain the level ground at the corner of the fence.

'I'll carry un, sir,' Turfrey grunted, 'if you'll bring the pack.'

He slung the unconscious King on his shoulders like a yoke and they retraced their way round the gorse-bushes, grateful for the intermittent shade of the trees, to the door in the wall,

Turfrey achieving a shambling trot over the whole distance. Ring went first through the doorway and peered round the corner of the barn. The carriage was standing there and he mentally blessed Madame Picart as he saw that she had harnessed two fresh horses. Beyond it the tree-shaded lane was still quiet and deserted, though from somewhere farther down it the shrill voices of children came to his ear. Less than ten minutes since he had been forced to plan afresh – another two minutes and they'd be away.

'In with him,' he told Turfrey. 'Then cast off. Do what you can for him,' he added over his shoulder to Jeanne as he ran for the cottage.

The key was in the door and he turned it, checking that it was locked. No sound came from within and he thought it best to make none himself. Turfrey, at the horses' heads, loosed them as soon as Ring had mounted to the box, and jumped inside as the carriage began to move. They turned into the lane, the horses snorting and tossing their heads under Ring's inexpert management, and a glance astern showed it empty in the direction of the Château. Where the narrow road passed into the shade of the tall forest trees four little girls were dancing on a patch of turf. Ring waved gaily to them. They would be able to tell the hunters which way the fox had gone but that couldn't damp his spirits at this moment.

For he was filled with a wild elation. He was away from Valençay with Ferdinand of Spain safely below decks, his course set for the French coast. He felt like a man who has unexpectedly performed a miracle. Then this foolish jubilation suddenly left him, and he was frowning as he took his whip and touched the horses into a canter. The French coast was fifty leagues away. It would be more than a miracle if they ever reached it.

VII

The Hurried Journey

1

The carriage had passed through Montrésor and was seven or eight miles beyond it before there was any sign of pursuit.

This long period of remission didn't greatly surprise Ring. As he urged his willing horses at the fastest speed his limited skill allowed he had had time to gauge it. At Valençay the folk in the Château would not at first suspect that the King had escaped; they would search for him, perhaps assuming that some whim had taken him exploring below the terraces, before wider inquiry was made. It could be an hour before the discovery of Madame Picart locked in her cottage and the report of the children at the roadside revealed that a carriage had taken the Montrésor road, and then horses had to be saddled and bridled before the hussars could give chase. None the less, he had driven for the last half-hour with his chin continually on his shoulder, watching for the small cloud of dust that would tell of horsemen coming up astern. There would have to be swift action when he saw it. He was resolved to stick to the carriage as long as possible before abandoning it, as much to give the King time to recover as to make the most of its speed.

They had emerged from the forest a mile or so from Montrésor without encountering another vehicle. A house in a wayside clearing, two women trudging towards the village; the parish priest and half-a-dozen children in Montrésor itself, a huddle of cottages below the wall of an ancient château; that was all they had seen of human life. Twice Jeanne had hailed him from the carriage window, shouting above the noise of wheels and hooves. The first time had been to tell him that

Madame Picart had left maize-cakes and a flask of wine in the carriage and that she was trying to revive Ferdinand with the wine, the second to report that the King had moved and groaned but had still not spoken or opened his eyes.

Now they were leaving an open countryside of orchards and cultivation and threading a way through woodland where the undulating road rarely afforded a view of the way they had come. It was fortunate that they were topping a slight rise when Ring, for the hundredth time looking over his shoulder, saw the moving wisp of reddish dust less than a mile away. At once he banged on the carriage roof and shouted.

'Stand by to abandon ship and take cover, Turfrey – see that the others are ready!'

He had three minutes at most. His plan was made but this was no place for it – beyond the roadside ditches the tangle of briars grew thick under the trees and made entry next to impossible. He whipped up the horses, rounded a bend, reined-in with all his strength as he saw the low stone parapets of a little bridge. It crossed a shallow brook a few feet wide that flowed leftward through the wood. Jeanne was out, then Turfrey lugging the King. Ring yelled to the seaman to get into the stream-bed and keep going, then drove on at a gallop. Beyond a second bend a hundred yards ahead he dragged the horses to a halt and jumped down, unhooked the pack which he had slung on the whip-socket, and ran back along the road as hard as he could go, wriggling into the straps of the pack as he went.

At the bend he saw no sign of the others and the road still clear. He ran on without stopping and had come within thirty paces of the bridge when the sudden clatter of hooves swiftly approaching sounded from beyond the next bend. He dived into the roadside ditch and lay flat among the weeds and tall grasses while the cavalcade thundered past so close that a spatter of gravel fell on his pack. They hadn't seen him. He raised himself cautiously in time to see them before they passed from sight: five blue-jacketed hussars, with sabres but no firearms that he could see. A moment later he heard their jubilant cries as they came upon the abandoned carriage.

Ring scrambled to his feet. His strategy was successful, as far as it went. The hussars would spend time searching the woods

near the carriage, time which the fugitives must use to get as far
away as possible. He stepped from the ditch into the roadway –
and saw, too late, the horseman who had just galloped into
view, the sixth hussar.

The man gave a hoarse shout and came hurtling down the
road, to rein-in with a sliding of hooves and fling himself off
his mount. By this time Ring had forced his way through the
barrier of briers and was a dozen paces into the wood,
trampling through the tall bracken that sprouted below the
branches of the oaks. If the man had sense enough to fetch his
comrades, he was thinking, escape would be impossible. He
snatched a backward glance through the bracken-fronds and
saw that the hussar was coming into the wood after him – he
couldn't know, of course, that the others were almost within
call. He would have to be dealt with, and quickly.

To his right one of the sessile oaks had fallen and its dead
branches offered an imperfect screen. Ring squatted behind it.
He slipped the pack from his shoulders and took from it the
knife he had used to threaten Gruvel. His left hand fell on a
thin branch in the grass beside him, dead but not yet rotten,
and he picked it up before writhing sideways to be clear of his
screen. The hussar was coming on, slashing a way through the
brambles with his sabre. Ring, crouching below the head-high
branch of an oak, saw his face through the network of foliage –
a young fellow, hardly more than a boy. He had to remind
himself that this was war, that the safety of three others beside
himself depended on the knife in his right hand.

The hussar halted a few paces away, peering left and right
over the bracken stems. His glance fell on Ring and with a
shout of '*Rendez-vous!*' he sprang forward, the sabre
half-raised. He saw the knife outthrust towards him and swept
up his weapon for a downward cut. Too late he perceived that
the oak-bough would intercept his blow, too late tried to
convert it into a thrust with the point. Ring's dead branch
easily deflected the thrust and at the same time he drove his
knife at the man's midriff with all his strength, feeling it sink in
to the full length of the blade. The hussar choked, dropped his
sabre, fell in a heap with blood gushing over the front of his
blue tunic.

Ring turned away, his mouth set in a hard line. He cleansed

the knife in the soft earth, put it in the pack, settled the pack on his shoulders and pushed on into the wood. This was no time for chivalry to a fallen foe. Before long his horse would be seen and his comrades would find him; dead or alive, he would show them which way Ring had gone. It couldn't be helped. There had been no alternative.

He hurried on at the fastest speed he could maintain, treading down the tangled undergrowth or skirting it where it grew too high, heading towards the sun that slanted its long lances through the canopy of leaves. The stream had been running north-west and sooner or later this course should intercept it. In five minutes he came to it and saw with satisfaction that a better route could hardly have been found for Jeanne and Turfrey and their helpless burden. The stream had carved for itself a broad ditch with sides waist-high in which a two-inch trickle of water idled over a bottom of small pebbles. He lowered himself into the stream-bed, spared a moment to swill the blood from his right hand, and began to make his way downstream.

The natural ditch ran almost straight and he made fast progress, ducking beneath overarching brambles, pausing twice to listen in vain for sounds of pursuit. A muddy footprint here and there showed that the others had passed that way, but not until clearer sunlight ahead marked the edge of the woodland did he hear a voice – Jeanne's voice – speaking as if in conversation. He climbed out onto the bank and saw her standing a yard or two away, her russet gown torn and bedraggled and spattered with mud, a loosened strand of hair clinging to her sunbrowned cheek. It could have been reaction from the recent violence that brought a ridiculous lump into his throat. She had been speaking to the King of Spain, who was lying on the ground with his back propped against a fallen treetrunk and his hands covering his face. Evidently he had regained his senses, for he groaned now and then. Beyond them the trees ended above a wide marsh of rushes and dwarf willow that stretched away to a distant strip of green where a few cattle grazed. There was no sign of Turfrey.

Jeanne turned her head as Ring stepped towards her and he saw the glad relief in her eyes.

'*Dieu merci*,' she whispered; and then more loudly, 'Robert, I have told his Majesty how we –'

'Good,' he cut in quickly. 'We've no time for talk, Jeanne. Where's Turfrey?'

'Gone to reconnoitre. But Robert – you must speak to the King.' She lowered her voice. 'He can walk if he wishes but he's said he'll go no farther. There's a great lump on the back of his head but I'm sure it's not serious.'

Ring nodded and stepped forward to stand above the recumbent man. He had managed to retain his hat and now he removed it; grinning inwardly as he did so at the thought that he was about to address the monarch by Divine Right of a country four times the size of England.

'Your Majesty, I am Robert Ring of his Britannic Majesty's Navy, at your Majesty's service. A British ship is waiting off the coast to take your Majesty back to Spain and we shall bring your Majesty to her.'

Ring stopped, aware of a proliferation of Majesties. Someone had told him that King George liked to be addressed as 'sir'. What was good enough for George the Third, he decided, was good enough for Ferdinand the Seventh.

'Bonaparte's soldiers are looking for us,' he went on rapidly, 'and we can't linger here. We shall win clear of them, monsieur, but only if you help us. You'll have to make an effort –'

'*Valga me Dios!*' Ferdinand flung his hands aside and sat up with a squeak of pain. 'Don't you see I'm badly hurt, man? I'm injured – ill – I need a doctor!' His French was fluent, with the vowels much stressed. 'Fetch a doctor, *imbécile*, a doctor!'

Remembering the fall he had witnessed, Ring felt some sympathy for him; the unattractive face that scowled up at him suggested an ill-tempered child rather than a man of twenty-seven, but he must be bruised and aching – probably with a splitting headache as well. He hardened his heart and bent forward, trying to find the right words.

'A doctor will attend you when you board the British ship, monsieur. To reach her will require the valour that was never wanting in the kings of Spain.' That might or might not be true; he sought for a peroration. 'Your throne is at stake, monsieur – your people wait for you to lead them to victory. All it needs is your will to go forward with us.'

And quickly, he added to himself. They were little more than half-a-mile from the road and the riderless horse. His words seemed to have had some effect at least. Though the King made no reply he remained sitting up, staring sullenly at Ring and biting his lip. Behind him Jeanne nodded approval – and suddenly Turfrey appeared noiselessly at her shoulder, a giant beside a pixie.

'So please ye, sir,' said Turfrey a trifle breathlessly, 'there's a river yonder, over where the kine are grazin'. No bridge. Farmhouse above t'other bank.'

'How wide's the river?'

'Didn't get near enough for a good look but I reckon we wouldn't swim across – not with him.' Turfrey jerked a thumb at the King, who was staring open-mouthed at this exchange in a foreign tongue. 'Flowin' sluggish-like but flowin' west, sir.'

Impossible, of course, that it should be the Loire – they must still be a score of miles from that. But undoubtedly this was a tributary.

'We might find good going along its bank,' he said, thinking aloud.

'Maybe, sir. But when I see this farmhouse on the one side, and farmer's kine on t'other, ho, thinks I, farmer'll have some kind o' ferry for when he –'

'A boat, by God!' Ring cut him short. 'We'll take a look for that, Turfrey.'

'Aye aye, sir. But it'd better be this side the river or we're out o' luck. I heard shoutin' on the far side o' the woods as I was comin' back.'

Another of those damned thin chances, Ring thought resignedly. He spoked rapidly in French telling Jeanne and the King of his intention. Ferdinand began a whining protest which ended in a Spanish oath as Turfrey hauled him unceremoniously to his feet and hooked one of the King's arms round his neck. Jeanne, meanwhile, was pulling from the seaman's capacious pockets the bottle of wine and bag of maize-cakes he had brought from the carriage and stowing them in Ring's pack. She spoke with sudden concern.

'There's blood on your sleeve, Robert.'

'I had to kill a man,' he said briefly. 'The more reason to hurry. – March!'

In five minutes, despite some rough ground where the King
– alternately swearing and whining – had to be carried bodily,
Turfrey's directions brought them round the edge of the
woodland to a place where they could see the river ahead and a
little below them. Rather less than a cable wide, Ring judged it,
its slow-moving surface unbroken by rock or rapid. Only a
short stretch of it was visible from where they stood, for a little
way downstream it curved out of sight between banks covered
with tall vegetation. They moved farther on and the farmhouse
came into view, a low greystone building half-buried in trees a
musket-shot above the river. And they saw the farmer's
'ferry-boat'. It was an enormous scow big enough to carry
half-a-dozen cattle, and it was tied up to a pole on the other
side of the river.

Ring accepted this setback with a gambler's philosophy.
Since its owners were on that side it had been long odds against
the boat's being on this. They would have to follow the river on
foot. He had opened his mouth to give the order to march
when Jeanne, who had parted the screen of leaves through
which they were peering, touched his arm and pointed. He saw
the second boat. It was a hundred yards downstream,
anchored in the middle of the shining river, and a
shock-headed lad in a blue shirt was sitting in it fishing. For an
instant Ring felt the poignancy of contrast between this scene
of utter peace and the bloody encounter in the wood; but it
was a fleeting instant and at once he was speaking fast, cutting
short a petulant complaint from Ferdinand.

'You'll have an easier passage in a moment, monsieur. –
Help him, Turfrey. No need to keep in cover.'

They scrambled down through bushes to the river bank. The
fisherman, who had his rod out over the stern and his back
towards them, turned to stare open-mouthed when Ring's
urgent hail reached him.

'*Holà*! We've an injured man here – will you put us across?
I'll pay you well.'

He held up a silver franc taken from his purse, turning it to
make it flash in the sunlight. The lad, a loutish youth of
fourteen or fifteen, hesitated only for a second. Then he took
in his rod, dropped a pair of sculls into the rowlocks, and
began to haul up his anchor. Nothing stirred near the

farmhouse above the opposite bank; but distant shouts came to Ring's ear from the woods and he knew that they had little time to spare. The boat was heading in towards the bank now, the boy standing up and pushing at the sculls. It was a slabsided ungainly craft but broad-beamed and capable of carrying half-a-dozen. He spoke from the corner of his mouth to Turfrey at his side.

'Take him when he lands. See that he doesn't cry out.'

The boat's forefoot nosed into the soft mud of the bank and the boy sprang ashore, to be caught in the enveloping clasp of Turfrey's arm with Turfrey's big hand clamped over his mouth. Ring fixed the goggling eyes with a ferocious glare.

'Make a sound and I'll throw you in the river. Keep quiet and you'll not be hurt. Understand?'

He helped the King into the bows, where he sank down on the wet anchor-rope with a groan; got the frightened boy into the sternsheets beside Jeanne and jumped in himself. Turfrey shoved off and scrambled aboard to squeeze onto the single midships thwart beside Ring. The heavy sculls dipped, the bow swung round, and they were pulling hard downstream towards the bend.

As he lugged at his oar, his work cut out to match Turfrey's mighty strokes, Ring's intent gaze shifted from one to the other of the danger-points they were leaving astern, the farmhouse on one bank and the wood on the other. If they were seen, the river would be worse than useless as an escape-route. They swept past the cattle grazing on the port side and began to round the curve of the stream. In the instant before the boat passed behind the screen of bushes that topped the left bank he thought he detected a movement at the edge of the wood where they had emerged from it, but there was no outcry to tell that they had been observed. Ahead of them the broad stream wound peacefully between its willow-fringed sides, and the waterfowl that scuttled into the reeds at their approach were the only signs of life. They held the fast stroke, making with the river's aid seven knots or more according to Ring's estimate, for another ten minutes. Then he handed over his scull to Turfrey and gave some attention to the King.

Ferdinand lay in an untidy heap in the bows with his eyes closed. Ring got the cloaks out of the pack and tucked them under the King's head and body, assuring him meanwhile that he was now safe from pursuit. His reward was to be sworn at, and the oath was followed by a querulous demand as to when they were going to arrive at the waiting ship. When Ring told him there would be two or three days of travel (an optimistic forecast, as he well knew) Ferdinand gave a moan of '*Dios mio!*' and buried his face in his arms. The man's state was perhaps not surprising; soft living was no preparation for the stunning fall he had sustained little more than three hours ago. But Ring sincerely hoped he would recover sufficient strength and spirit to look after himself.

While Turfrey's apparently inexhaustible strength drove the boat on, Jeanne with a great deal of patience had extracted some information from the scared lad beside her. This river was the Indre, it appeared, and joined the Loire a few leagues above Saumur. How many leagues it was to the junction of rivers the boy didn't know but thought it might be eight or nine. There were no rapids that he knew of, though he'd heard there were a lot of sandbanks where it entered the larger river, and there were bridges at Montbazon and Azay-le-Rideau. Ring consulted the crude map provided by the Compagnie des Diligences d'Anjou, from which he made out that if and when they reached the Loire they would be at least a dozen miles west of Tours.

The comfort of being afloat once more was so stimulating that for a moment he considered using the boat to make more westerly distance down the Loire itself. But the extra risk far outbalanced the extra speed. News of the King's escape would travel as fast or faster than they could – horsemen would be galloping to Saumur and Angers and the Loire would become a trap. The north bank of the Loire and then a cross-country journey in whatever cover they might find; that was the only course for them.

In the next two hours they passed half-a-dozen people fishing from the banks and two boats pulling upstream, exchanging nods and casual waves of the hands. Twice they saw the spires and rooftops of villages above the wooded slopes of the right bank, but the left bank seemed to be mostly swampy wilderness. It was on this side that they put the boy ashore a little after sunset, with the silver franc and one of Ring's remaining three gold napoleons in his pocket. Night had fallen when they passed beneath the first bridge, unchallenged and apparently unnoticed; and in a dark and lonely reach a mile farther on Ring, who was pulling, shipped his sculls and they shared the wine and maize-cakes Madame Picart had provided, Ferdinand receiving his portion without comment and thereafter retiring into silence. Then on again, warily, down the glimmering water under the stars.

With Ring and Turfrey spelling each other at the sculls they made steady progress all that night, with no accidents except a harmless collision with a drifting snag and the passage of a low weir. The few houses of Azay-le-Rideau, on the right bank, rose grey and silent in the dawn half-light as the boat glided like a shadow under its bridge. An hour later it emerged from the mists that writhed among the maze of sandy islets at the mouth of the Indre into the wide slow-flowing Loire.

On the farther shore a corner of forest came down almost to the river bank. Ring and Turfrey, pulling across the current, beached their craft below the trees and the four clambered up the bank and crossed the rough track that ran above it. There was a clump of conifers fifty yards inside the wood and on the mattress of pine-needles they lay down to rest. Ring, lowering himself with a sigh of relief, found that Jeanne had placed herself so that his head rested in her lap. In a matter of seconds he was asleep.

2

The big taproom of the Lion d'Angers was crowded with men, packed to its doors, its atmosphere thick with the odours of damp clothing and horse. Outside in the field behind the inn horses were being led or galloped in the lingering mists of the autumn morning; and the ceaseless din of voices indoors was largely concerned with the striking of bargains. The horse fair was the life and *raison d'être* of the little village that had grown up round the inn and taken its name, and fair days meant money – and hard work – to the innkeeper and his men who were just now very busy round the row of casks at the inner end of the room. The innkeeper glanced up irritably at the man who had just forced his way through the crowd and was demanding his attention.

'If you want cider you'll wait your turn,' he said with a scowl.

'I don't want your cider, my good man,' returned the newcomer shortly. 'I want a carriage.'

The innkeeper stooped to fill a tankard from the tap. 'Then you've come to the wrong market. It's horses they're selling here. Maybe you thought all those carriages outside my inn were for sale, eh? Well, they're the carriages of my customers, here to buy horses.' He handed the brimming tankard to a serving-man and turned a questioning stare on the man who confronted him: a middle-sized man in a round hat, coat mud-spattered, linen none too clean. 'You're a stranger in these parts, it seems. Where from?'

'I don't like impertinence, my friend,' said the other, gently but with an undertone of steel. 'If you must know, I come from Redon and my name is Robert Laval. Even you, I think, will have heard of the Montfort-Lavals.'

The innkeeper gulped. 'Of course, monsieur. I trust monsieur will pardon –'

'*Pas d'importance.* The state of my clothes excuses you. Attend to me, now. My carriage is overturned in a ditch on the Châteauneuf road, my coachman has ridden into Angers to fetch assistance.'

'No one hurt, monsieur, I trust?'

'My cousin hurt his leg but only slightly. He, and my sister and manservant, were travelling with me to Châteaubriant, where I must be before noon to attend a meeting of magistrates. I require a carriage to get me there. You understand?'

Monsieur Laval from Redon produced a bulging leather purse as he spoke and displayed, momentarily, the gold coin he took from it. The innkeeper ducked his head.

'It may perhaps be arranged,' he said. 'Monsieur's party is here?'

'They are approaching up the road. I walked ahead. Will you see to the matter at once?'

The innkeeper, fingering his chin, darted a questing glance round the noisy room. 'If monsieur will await me here,' he said, and ploughed his way into the throng.

Ring replaced the purse in his pocket. In addition to two napoleons and five francs it contained a lot of pebbles. The appearance of affluence and the sound of a good family name, he was thinking, seemed to have turned the trick – and that was just as well. For he had to have that carriage.

Two days had passed since they had crossed the Loire and in those two days they had covered thirty miles on foot. First northward by forest tracks, where Turfrey's country-bred sagacity and Ring's sense of direction supplemented Jeanne's guidance (for she could only tell them that they must head north to be clear of Angers) and then westward into open countryside of hilly fields and lonely farms. The first night they had found shelter with a community of woodcutters, who fed them and gave them a draughty log-shed to sleep in; a franc from Ring's dwindling store had disarmed their questions.

The second day and weather that threatened rain found them entering a land of copses and pools and small winding rivers where progress was difficult and secret progress impossible. Sometimes the streams could be forded but to cross the larger ones they had to find the highway and use the bridge. Thus they crossed the Loir at Durtal, walking boldly through the litle village under its tall château and even pausing to buy bread. No one questioned their passage; even the lad from whom Jeanne asked the name of his village only stared and wagged his head in astonishment that anyone should be so ignorant. Durtal gave Jeanne her bearings. Angers lay four leagues to the south, she told them; if they could cross the Angers-Laval road before nightfall they could be in her own Brittany by the next evening, perhaps reach the mill at Callac the following night. The mill at Callac had become the goal and Mecca of this hurried pilgrimage. Once there they would find a known friend to help them and speed them on their way. And it was only a day's march from Callac to Erdeven and the sea. The obstacle to their getting there was the King of Spain.

Ring had been amazed at the change in Ferdinand's behaviour. After their few hours of sleep in the forest above the Loire the King had indeed begun with oaths and surly protests, but within an hour he was marching resolutely if sullenly, keeping (though with difficulty) his two paces behind Turfrey.

Ring soon perceived that Jeanne's presence was responsible for this. Ferdinand's vanity was asserting itself as the effects of his fall wore off and it would not let him appear unmanly before a pretty woman. Jeanne had been quick to see and use this, prodding him to fresh efforts with a shrug or a curl of the lip when he showed signs of faltering. But vanity, however potent, couldn't cure his blistered feet. The light shoes he was wearing were quite unsuited to rough walking. At the end of the first day he was limping heavily, and so far from crossing the Angers-Laval road on the second they were forced at nightfall to seek shelter at a lonely farm two miles short of it. Here Jeanne contrived to win the sympathy of the farmer's wife, who not only let them sleep in a barn but also sold them – for one of Ring's few silver francs – a pair of her husband's old shoes. In these, when Jeanne had stuffed them with pieces torn from her petticoat, the King could shuffle slowly and painfully with Turfrey's help; too slowly for Ring, who determined to find some way of recovering their lost ground. Their emergence on the road half-a-mile from a village, and Jeanne's remark that if they could get as far as Châteaubriant they would be in Brittany, had given him his cue.

He was wondering now, as he waited in the crowded taproom of the Lion d'Angers, whether the hue-and-cry after the missing King of Spain had reached Châteaubriant.

The innkeeper, shoving and cursing, came back through the press of drinkers with a ruddy-faced man at his heels. Pierre Messac, he said, would take monsieur and his party to Châteaubriant – had stayed overnight at the inn and was returning this morning to his farm on the other side of the town – had already put-to his horses so monsieur would not have to wait. It would cost monsieur three napoleons.

Ring raised his eyebrows. 'If Monsieur Messac is going to Châteaubriant in any case one napoleon is ample,' he said loftily.

'Two, *alors*,' Pierre Messac said quickly. 'As a favour to monsieur – two napoleons.'

'How far is it to Châteaubriant?'

'Six leagues, monsieur.'

'Very well.'

Ring had seen Turfrey looking in through the door at the

other end of the room. He handed two napoleons to Messac and with lordly indifference dropped two silver francs into the innkeeper's ready palm. His money (the Baron de Feriet's money, he suddenly remembered) was now reduced to three francs. He followed Messac outside, where seven or eight vehicles – carts, wagons, gigs – stood along the inn wall in the light rain that had begun to fall. Two or three men who lounged against the wheels with horsecloths draped over their shoulders were taking little notice of the three cloaked figures standing near the door.

Ring nodded in response to the anxious question Jeanne's eyes flashed at him from beneath her hood and beckoned them into Messac's wake. He saw with some dismay that Messac's vehicle was a light wagonette without a hood; and wondered whether, as one of the Montfort-Lavals, he ought to make an angry protest. He compromised by scowling as the man, with apologies for the lack of shelter, assisted them to board.

'The rain will pass in half-an-hour,' he added. 'Monsieur will see.'

He climbed to the box-seat, flourished his whip, and the wagonette clattered off, its two spirited horses pulling as if they knew they were heading for their home stable. The passengers sat two-a-side on the high bench-seats, facing each other. Ring grinned at Jeanne.

'Not as comfortable as our own luxurious carriage, my dear,' he said, 'but at least it's taking us to Châteaubriant.'

Her answering smile changed to a frown. 'You've no cloak, Robert, and you're getting wet.'

'I do very well, I thank you.'

'You'll do as your sister bids you,' she said severely. 'You are not the only one who can make plans.' She lowered her voice. 'I must do what I can for those blistered feet while we have the chance. *Ça s'arrange.*'

She made the King take off his cloak and sit on the floor of the wagonette with his back against the inner end, then gave her own cloak to Ring to put on. Obeying her instructions, Ring and Turfrey stretched the third cloak tightly between them, making a canopy beneath which she could crouch in shelter while she removed Ferdinand's shoes; it also sheltered Ferdinand, except for his head which projected wearing a comical expression of mingled wrath and offended dignity. The improvised sick-berth had not been rigged more than five minutes when Messac called over his shoulder from the box-seat.

'Monsieur! Do you see these lads ahead of us?'

Ring leaned out to look at the road in front. It ran straight here, undulating gently down and up again for half-a-mile. Three horsemen, all clad alike in dark-blue cloaks and cocked hats, appeared on the crest of the opposing slope, riding towards them.

'*Gens-d'armes-à-cheval*,' the farmer shouted above the noise of wheels and hooves. 'Came into Châteaubriant yesterday morning from Blois. Looking for that Fernando, the Spanish king, they are – seems he's got away from Valençay.'

Ring hastily signed to Turfrey to crouch and pull the hood of his cloak round his face. Beneath the spread cloak he felt Jeanne's hand clutch his ankle tightly in token that she had heard.

'Indeed?' he said, feigning indifference.

'*C'est vrai*, monsieur. I saw them nailing up a notice on the door of the hôtel de ville.'

There'd be a description, mention – at the least – of three men and a woman. Ferdinand's appearance and features might be described. Yet Messac apparently had no suspicion of his passengers.

'And what did this notice say?' he inquired as casually as he could.

'*Sais pas*, monsieur. I was driving out on my way to the Lion d'Angers and didn't stop.'

Messac was slowing his horses for the downhill slope, the gendarmes riding up it at walking pace. In thirty seconds they would meet. Ring jammed his hat hard down over the King's head and face as Messac called a cheerful greeting.

'*Ohé, messieurs* – got your man yet?'

'No.'

'Well, you won't find him at the Lion. I've just come from there.'

Messac was not pulling up. Ring stared woodenly at the three as they passed, hunched under the falling rain, red-striped breeches showing beneath dripping cloaks. Only one of them spared a cursory glance for the two hooded figures in the wagonette with a cloak spread across their knees and a hat resting on the cloak, and there was no backward glance as they were left behind. With a muttered apology Ring pulled the hat from Ferdinand's face, which showed no sign of fright and wore so peculiar an expression that Ring suddenly wondered whether he would have welcomed discovery.

'How much farther?' was all the King said in his usual grumbling whine.

Jeanne answered from under the cloak, her voice lowered to prevent Messac from hearing. 'Ten leagues from Châteaubriant to Callac, then six to Erdeven and the sea, your Majesty. In three days your Majesty will be safe on board a British ship.'

'Sixteen leagues! *Dios mio!*' It was a moan.

'I shall put on your Majesty's other shoe, if you please.' Ferdinand gave a yelp, which was disregarded. 'There – walking will be more comfortable now. It will need courage, but I know your Majesty has abundance of that. Tonight we shall find good lodging with friends in the Gavrain forest, only four leagues from Châteaubriant. You see, we are in my own country here and I know it well.'

Ferdinand's only reply was to wince as his invisible nurse made some adjustment to his bandagings. Ring, observing him covertly, noted a certain wildness in the twitching of the sallow features and the rapid shifting of the bloodshot eyes. Of course the man was undergoing a physical trial far more severe than it was for his companions, each of whom, including Jeanne, was accustomed to hard work in hard conditions. Would his sufferings tip the balance against the distant prospect of regaining his throne? He had heard what Messac said; he must realise that all he had to do to return to the easy life at Valençay was to leap from the wagonette in Châteaubriant and proclaim his identity. It was very plain that they must not risk entering Châteaubriant – but how could they avoid doing so without arousing the farmer's suspicions?

The rain had stopped and a gleam of watery sunshine lit the wide landscape of low hills and woodlands. They were approaching a village and Ring made Jeanne stay beneath the cloak-canopy until they were past. The gendarmes had passed through here; the villagers might well be on the lookout for three men and a woman.

'St Julien,' Messac threw over his shoulder. 'Châteaubriant in twenty minutes, monsieur. They hold the Tribunal d'Instance in the hôtel de ville,' he added, 'so I will set monsieur down there, if he pleases.'

'Do so,' Ring replied with a sinking heart.

They'd have to disembark at the very door where that damned notice proclaimed them as wanted fugitives – in a *Place*, no doubt, busy with townspeople who'd read it. Fool that he'd been to talk about attending a meeting of magistrates! Turfrey had hoisted Ferdinand back onto his seat and Jeanne was speaking to the King, encouraging and flattering him. Ring cudgelled his brains to find some excuse for leaving the wagonette before they came into Châteaubriant. He was only too well aware how thin was the story he had told and how probable it was that Messac thought it somewhat odd; simply to order the man to pull up, tell him they preferred to walk the rest of the way – two gentlefolk with a servant and a cousin with an injured leg – would be beyond belief. He had still found no solution when Châteaubriant came into sight half-a-mile ahead.

It was a small town dominated by a mediaeval castle-keep, its grey roofs packed within half-ruined city walls. The road, bordered with trees and bushes, ran almost to the stone gateway leading into the town before the first houses appeared. Ring received inspiration in the nick of time. He spoke quickly in Jeanne's ear.

'When we stop, get out in a great hurry and run behind the bushes on the left of the road. Hide yourself.'

She stared her astonishment. 'Why?'

'For decency's sake, *chérie*.' Ring stood up suddenly and shouted. 'Monsieur Messac! Stop – please stop at once!'

His tone was urgent and the farmer was reining-in before he spoke. 'What is it, monsieur?'

'*Mademoiselle ma soeur* –' Ring whispered the rest. 'Impossible to wait a moment longer,' he ended.

Messac grinned. '*Entendu*, monsieur.'

The horses trampled to a halt a musket-shot from the town gate. A cottage stood among trees a few yards ahead but between it and the wagonette the bushes grew tall and thick at the roadside. At Ring's gesture Turfrey sprang over the tailboard to help Jeanne as she clambered down with a show of flustered urgency. She scuttled into the bushes. After much rustling and crackling, which seemed to indicate that she was not finding it easy to get into concealment, there was silence. Ring had got out and was helping Ferdinand to descend.

'We will not detain you, Monsieur Messac,' he said off-handedly. 'I am obliged for the use of your wagonete.'

'I can wait, monsieur,' Messac protested. 'Your cousin –'

'Two minutes' walk will ease my cousin's stiffness and I have time to spare before my meeting. Adieu, Monsieur Messac, and thank you.'

Ring turned away as if you speak to his cousin. After a moment the farmer shrugged and shook his reins and the wagonette passed on. Ring waited until it had vanished into the street beyond the gate before calling to Jeanne, who emerged smiling from behind the bushes. She cut his apologetic explanation short.

'As it chanced,' she said primly, 'it was not inconvenient. But if we are to walk, Robert, we had better start now.'

There had been no one in the vicinity of the wagonette when it set them down but now there were two or three people coming out through the town gate.

'Westward,' Ring said. 'But by what route –'

'To the left beyond the cottage. It's the road to Nantes but we'll not follow it for long.'

She led the way. Ring and Turfrey each took one of Ferdinand's arms, ignoring his protests, and hurried him round the corner into the side-road. There was no outcry to tell that they had been observed from the town gate, and the road at once bent to the right between narrow flanking belts of hazel-trees with fields of maize stretching away beyond them.

'It's long since I was here,' Jeanne said a little anxiously, 'but I think – ah, this is our way.'

She had found a gap where a rutted track through the hazel thickets on the right led across the maize field between the head-high stems. As they turned into it Turfrey spoke.

'So please ye, sir, we could do with a staff apiece and there's good uns here. Ten minutes 'd do it.'

Ring nodded and they released the King, who sank down in

despondent silence. Turfrey took the big knife from the pack and set about selecting and cutting four stout staffs from the straight hazel saplings that sprouted under the larger trees, while Jeanne explained what she proposed. The path through the maize would bring them in half-a-league to the farm of St Aubin, which they would have to pass in order to gain the tracks leading westward through the forest of Teillay. Once beyond the Vilaine, which they must cross by the little bridge of Port-de-Roch, they would enter the wild country of the *landes*. There, in the Gavrain forest, was the old house of Bernuit where the family of Melard lived, old friends of her father and devoted royalists; it was seven years since she had visited them but they would remember her and give them food and shelter. And tomorrow morning an early start, for it was not far short of six leagues to Callac.

'You'll have to trust to my guidance now, Robert,' she ended, with a sudden smile that held something of apology. 'I'm in my own country at last.'

He looked at her in silence for a moment; her russet gown torn and bedraggled, shoes and stockings splashed with mud, she stood erect and confident as if they were carefree holidaymakers instead of hunted fugitives. There couldn't be another girl like her in the wide world, he told himself, remembering the toils and hazards they had faced together. A random sunbeam struck through the low clouds and glinted on the braided coils of hair, touching to beauty the smooth lines of cheek and brow. At the frank admiration of his glance her own eyes fell and she coloured faintly. Ring took a step forward.

'Jeanne,' he began.

'I am hungry!' the King interrupted impatiently, hauling himself stiffly to his feet. '*Valga me Dios!* When am I to eat?'

Jeanne turned to him quickly. 'When we reach Bernuit, your Majesty shall have good food and a good bed. But we have four leagues to march first. Your Majesty has managed so bravely thus far,' she added with a flattering glance, 'that he will march as gallantly as any of us.'

Ferdinand grunted ungraciously and accepted without a word the hazel staff which Turfrey put into his hand. Ring nodded approval. In the pack were the crusts of bread remaining from the frugal breakfast provided by the farmer's wife, but these had better be kept in reserve; they had twelve miles to go before they reached Bernuit and its plentiful supplies. Turfrey shouldered the pack and they started along the narrow passage through the maize, the King unassisted and at first limping heavily but soon walking with a resolution that Ring had not thought him capable of.

The sound of a bell striking the hour of noon came distantly to their ears as they came in sight of the long low buildings of the farm. Men were out on the vast golden plain harvesting the maize, too far away for even a shouted greeting, and they passed the farm without seeing anyone else. A rough track led onward, mounting slightly towards a broken horizon of little hills that rose against the clouded western sky, and behind them the castle-keep of Châteaubriant slowly diminished beyond a flat patchwork of green and brown. When they gained the cover of a fringe of stunted oaktrees Ring paused for a long backward glance. There was no sign of any pursuit and he had scarcely expected any. They had yet again won a clear start – and the worst part of the journey was done.

A thin rain began to drift in their faces, a cold rain that reminded him that summer was gone and autumn upon them, but it couldn't damp his rising spirits. He saw in his mind's eye the dark line of the sea, the blaze of a fire on desolate Erdeven Point, *Implacable*'s boat pulling in to take them off. In sixty hours more that vision could become reality.

3

And through the rest of that day the rain persisted, never increasing to a downpour but maintaining its falling veil of moisture beneath the low dark skies. Ring had peremptorily refused to accept Turfrey's cloak, but before they had emerged from the Teillay woods the three cloaked pilgrims were as wet as their uncloaked leader. On so dark and damp an afternoon there were few folk about, and an old farm labourer with a sack over his head was the only man they met in the narrow horse-paths west of the woodlands. He spared them no more than a grunt as they passed and went on his way without a backward glance for the oddly-assorted party of wayfarers: the pretty brown-faced girl and her cloakless escort, the big man and the little man behind them, all grasping staffs and walking the miry track at a curiously leisurely pace compared with the old farmer's.

Their slow pace was because of the King. Ferdinand had risen considerably in Ring's estimation by the gameness he had showed in the first half-hour after leaving Châteaubriant. With his thick lower lip jutting like the bows of a schooner he had stepped it out manfully despite his blistered feet, never once demanding assistance or grumbling at the rate they were going. Rain trickled down across his pale grimly-set features, mud clogged his shoes (from which strips torn from Jeanne's petticoat protruded) and still he held the steady pace Ring was setting. But this display of courage, or perhaps of inherited Hapsburg stubbornness, lasted no more than thirty minutes. At a steepening of the rough path Ferdinand flung down his staff and declared with tears in his voice that he could not go a step further. It took much patient encouragement from Ring, and a highly-coloured account of Bernuit's luxuries from Jeanne, to get him moving again; and then it was at a much slower pace and a good deal of help from Turfrey. The King seemed to have accepted the big seaman as his personal servant and beast of burden, while Turfrey took the oaths and unintelligible orders that came his way with a grinning equanimity. Without this unequal partnership they would never have reached the bridge over the Vilaine before nightfall.

A farm track brought them to the river in the gloom of late afternoon. It was a shallow stream here, and they could have forded it without taking the slight risk of using the bridge or (as Turfrey remarked) getting any wetter than they already were. But the bridge was narrow and led only to a track on the opposite bank where two cottages stood silent and lifeless, and they crossed it and toiled slowly up a path behind the cottages, mounting the stony flank of a hill towards a ragged crest of forest. The ascent was rough, the rocks that protruded here and there slippery with rain, and Ring and Turfrey had to haul the King bodily up the steeper places. When they halted to rest in the trees at the top of the ascent Jeanne gave them encouragement.

'The forest path will lead us into the road that runs to the house of Bernuit,' she said. 'in less than an hour we shall be there.'

The ring of confidence in her tone stimulated Ferdinand to a final effort and they marched steadily if slowly along the winding path between the trees. Ring himself was beginning to tire. Above the canopy of leaves and boughs the early dusk was seeping into the curtain of falling rain and under the trees it was almost dark; the dripping forest, the dank chill, and the prisoning tree-boles repelled him.

For the first time he felt a pang of yearning for the sea with its limitless freedom of movement, a wave of hatred for the enclosing horizons of the land. He found himself sniffing futilely to catch some faint breath of the salt, and grinned wryly at his folly; the nearest sea was thirty miles away, and the odours of wet vegetation and rotting wood were all that came to his nostrils.

In front of him on the path Turfrey, lugging the King through the dead foliage of a fallen tree, growled an English oath – the first he had let fall since their travels began. Jeanne, a dim figure flitting through the gloom ahead, stumbled and almost fell. Yes, they were all weary. And soaked to the skin, and hungry. It was well that they were coming to a place of warmth and light and food.

For half-an-hour, while the darkness grew until the falling rain was no longer visible, the path wound through the forest, in places so faint that Ring thought it must be very rarely used. Then, quite suddenly, the trees fell back and they had joined a broader track coming from the north. The timber had been cleared from a few yards each side of it and it had once been metalled and smooth, but now grass had grown over the metalling and dead branches sprawled across its surface. Jeanne, Ring saw, was hurrying on faster than her followers; beyond her there was a lightening of the twilight that must indicate an open space, a clearing. She was a hundred paces ahead when she halted as if turned to stone.

Ring overtook Turfrey and the King and ran to join her. Before he reached her side he saw what she was looking at. There was a wide clearing, grey and desolate; a tangle of vegetation that might once have been a garden; beyond this the ruin of a house, its roof fallen and its naked timbers blackened by fire.

Jeanne turned as he came up. 'Bernuit,' she said tremulously, 'the Melards – gone. And I told you –'

Ring caught and held her tightly against him as a burst of sobbing ended her utterance. 'You told us you were here seven years ago, *chérie*,' he said firmly. 'You could not foretell this. And at least there should be some kind of shelter over yonder.'

'I will look.' She freed herself quickly. 'Soon it will be too dark to see.'

She went towards the ruin. Ring waited to hail Turfrey, who was all but carrying the drooping Ferdinand as the two came slowly on.

'The house is burnt out, a ruin,' he said briskly. 'We'll have to make the best of it. Bring him along.'

He followed Jeanne, skirting the overgrown garden. Two minutes' inspection sufficed to show that Bernuit had not a square yard of sheltering roof remaining. Its upper storey had no doubt been of timber, and all that was left was an oblong of ruined walls enclosing a chaos of broken stone and rotting wood. It was Jeanne who found the stone embrasure of the hearth with its sheltering ingles; rain was coming down the shattered aperture of the chimney but four people could crouch on either side in comparative shelter. Ring called to Turfrey and the King was brought in across the piled rubbish to be dumped like a sack in one corner of the hearth; whether by reason of utter fatigue or sheer misery, he made no complaint but slumped down with his head on his chest and his eyes closed. While Ring and Jeanne did what they could for his comfort Turfrey muttered something and disappeared, to return after a few minutes and beckon his commanding officer outside.

'Reckon I've found a brace o' cabins for them as ain't too particular, sir,' he said, leading the way along a paved path at the back of the ruin.

It was still just light enough to make out what had once been an enclosure for animals or fowls amid the tall weeds. It had been thirty or forty feet long and at either end of it was a stone structure no higher than a man's waist and looking rather like a tomb. These fowl-houses (for such they must have been) were roofed with heavy slabs on which the grass had grown and had narrow door-openings in their sides. Ring, on hands and knees, squeezed in through the opening of the nearer one. There had been litter of hay or straw inside, but the years had disintegrated it and whatever droppings it held into a floor of soft granules. This floor was as dry as a bone.

'Turfrey,' he said, backing out again, 'you're a jewel.'

'Thankee, sir. T'other's same as this.'

'Very well, then. It's damned close quarters for two but we'll need all the warmth we can muster. You'll have to be gentleman of the bedchamber to the King of Spain, Turfrey, and bodyguard too. We can't put him in here by himself, so –'

Ring caught himself up abruptly as the implication of this arrangement struck him. There wasn't as much as four feet width in the 'cabins'. To get a third man in with Turfrey and Ferdinand was physically impossible.

'Aye aye, sir,' said Turfrey imperturbably. 'And by'r leave, sir, we'd best eat our scraps and turn in afore it's pitch-black.'

They made their way back and scrambled over the wet rubble to the meagre shelter of the hearth. Jeanne turned from speaking to the King as they crouched in out of the rain.

'I've explained to his Majesty that this ill fortune will be amply repaid when we reach the mill at Callac tomorrow,' she said with a meaning look at Ring. 'His Majesty has most gallantly declared that he can endure another day's travel.'

'I shall try,' Ferdinand muttered sullenly.

'Bravo, monsieur!' Ring's praise was sincere. 'And at least you'll sleep dry tonight, for Turfrey here has found a better lodging than this. But we'll sup first.'

Jeanne shared out the few damp crusts from the pack; they were all hungry enough to finish this wretched supper to the last crumb. While they ate Ring told of the discovery of the 'cabins'.

'They've no merit but dryness,' he added to Jeanne, 'but one is for you. The King has the other with Turfrey to keep him company.'

'And you?' she said quickly.

'I shall do very well here with a cloak to cover me.' He stood up. 'We'll start at daybreak tomorrow so the sooner we turn in the better.'

Jeanne did not speak while they were assisting Ferdinand through the rain and darkness to his cramped lodging, getting him inside, and arranging him so that Turfrey could lie across the door-opening. She followed Ring in silence to the other end of the enclosure, waited in silence while he stooped to make sure that the floor was dry. As he straightened himself she spoke suddenly.

'I'm wet to the skin, Robert. I'm shivering with cold. So was the King. He's to have another's warmth to help him – I'm to have none, it seems.'

'You'll be warmer once you're in there,' he said awkwardly. 'I'll find a way to fix your cloak over the door –'

'*Dieu-de-dieu!* And shut me in with – perhaps – a rat or a snake? I will not spend the night in there alone, Monsieur Robert Ring!' He thought she stamped her foot, but it was now too dark to see. 'Either you'll be gracious enough to lend me your company or I'll lend you mine in that miserable ruin.' Her voice changed from anger to pleading. 'Robert – I'm *cold.*'

She turned from him and crawled in through the opening. After a second's hesitation he followed her. There was room to lie at full length but of necessity their bodies touched. Hers was indeed shivering. Ring put his arms round her.

'That is better,' she whispered. 'But – to be warm – we should be – closer yet.'

In the darkness his lips found hers. She made no protest when he began to undo the lacing of her bodice, and after a moment her fingers came to assist him.

Over the forest clearing the night clouds shed the last of their rain and in a little while a star winked clear. It would be a fine day tomorrow.

VIII

The Mill at Callac

1

Jean Kerzo's mill had been built by his great-grandfather in the time of Louis XIV, a hundred years before the misdeeds of the Revolution made a Chouan of Jean. It lay in a small valley where two large pools, one higher than the other, formed an open space in the wilderness of tangled woodland and heathery crags. The stone mill-house with its overshot wheel stood beside the mill-stream at the lower end of the pools, its long outhouses sheltering the miller's wagons and horses and the forest hemming it in on every side. Remote and solitary though it was, a wagon-road constructed with immense labour twisted uphill from it through rocks and thickets to join a wider lane several miles away, by which the miller could transport his flour to Vannes or even to Port-Louis on the sea-coast.

At the first steep zigzag of the wagon-road above the mill a forest path descended to join it, and down this path through the chequered shadows of late afternoon came a weary party of four.

It was the fifth day of that hurried journey from Valençay, and they had covered eighteen miles on foot since daybreak. Jeanne, whose knowledge of the path had guided them all day, was the first to reach the wider track and look down on the mill just below; tired though she was, she showed less fatigue than the others, for Ring and Turfrey between them had borne all the toil of assisting the exhausted King of Spain. Turfrey, indeed, had carried Ferdinand on his back for the last hour and even his seemingly inexhaustible strength was nearly at an end.

Jeanne turned a smiling face to her followers. 'All's well!' she called. 'The mill-house – and smoke coming from its chimney.'

Ring helped Turfrey to get the King down the steep bank into the lane and then went to join her. Below the slope of hazels he saw the mill-race, the motionless wheel, the long building that was half mill and half dwelling-house, all in shadow now; beyond the stables and barns the lower mill-pond spread a sheet of blue between its fringing walls of woodland. Nothing stirred; the only sound was the cheerful song of the mill-race. No scene could have been more peaceful, or – to dog-tired travellers – so suggestive of rest and food.

'And tomorrow,' he said, half to himself, 'the sea at last. And the ship.' He rubbed his bristly chin. 'I must shave tonight – if I can stay awake long enough.'

'And I must find myself a new gown,' Jeanne said. 'Perhaps Madame Kerzo will help me, though indeed she is twice my size.'

Ring turned to look at her. There had been no opportunity for talk between them all day, for when he woke at first light she had gone from their shelter to wash in a stream and after that they had been with Turfrey and the King. Strangely (as it seemed to him) the new relationship engendered last night had not altered her manner towards him; that they had been lovers had brought no change in her happy comradeship. It occurred to Ring that he had a great deal yet to learn about Jeanne Bonchamps. He was about to speak when Turfrey, who had left his burden propped against the bank, joined them and bent a frowning scrutiny upon the mill and its neighbourhood.

'Looks quiet enough, sir,' Turfrey said dubiously. 'Howsomever, I'd best go down first and take a look, by'r leave, sir.'

'We'll all go down,' Ring said impatiently. 'I'll help you with the King.'

His impatience had been roused some way back along the path when Turfrey suddenly asserted that they were being watched and began to halt and listen intently every few paces. Ring had been short with him. If there was anyone hiding in the thickets it was probably poachers – poachers didn't want to be seen, as Turfrey should know, he had added unkindly. Turfrey had held his peace while continuing to peer about him. And now, as they started down the hill, the two men supporting Ferdinand between them, his suspicious glance questioned the bushes and thickets that bordered the track. From behind them Jeanne spoke confidently for the King's benefit.

'Your Majesty will find that all our troubles are over now. Jean Kerzo the miller fought for King Louis and will do all he can to help us. Your Majesty must remember that your arrival won't be expected, also that the miller and his wife are plain folk –'

'There will be food?' Ferdinand broke in with more liveliness that he had shown all day.

'Of course, your Majesty – plain food, but in plenty.'

'*Muy bien*,' grunted his Majesty. 'I am exceedingly hungry.'

They had reached the wide low bridge over the mill-stream, some distance from the mill-house. Crossing it, they advanced towards a spacious yard with the house on one side fronting a rank of big stables and barns on the other. A muffled barking of dogs sounded from somewhere behind the barns, but no one came out from the stone porch of the house. The high woods standing against the western sky cast their dark shadow over Callac and only the farther end of the lake, visible beyond, still shone blue under the westering sun. With an abruptness that gave no time for his usual 'by'r leave, sir' Turfrey left the King to his commander's care and trotted noiselessly over to the stables. He was back in a moment, his eyes glancing suspiciously to left and right as he spoke low-voiced to Ring.

'Thought I see a carriage through a gap yonder, sir. It's there right enough, behind the stables. An' nigh on a dozen hosses in them stables.'

'It's a well-kept house and Kerzo must be a man of means,' Ring said shortly. 'No reason why he shouldn't keep a carriage.'

They had reached the porch, a massive stone projection flanked by ancient yews which almost hid its walls. He went in, Jeanne and Turfrey with the King close behind him, and banged with his fist on the oaken door. A man's voice called gruffly '*Entrez!*' He lifted the latch and was on the point of stepping over the threshold when there was a sudden scuffle behind him, an oath from Turfrey and a cry from Jeanne. Before he could turn an unseen hand thrust him violently forward to plunge headfirst through the doorway into the room beyond. He landed sprawling, started to get up, and halted on his knees, staring. A man was sitting at the table facing him. High-bridged nose, side-whiskers, narrow bright eyes. Ring had seen them a fortnight ago in *Nonpareil*'s cabin.

'Francis Verlay, by God!' he said hoarsely.

2

'François Labiche, *s'il vous plaît*,' said the man at the table coolly.

The outer door slammed and the key was turned in the lock. Twisting round as he scrambled to his feet, Ring saw that Jeanne and Turfrey had been thrust inside with him. Of the King there was no sign.

'See here, Mr Verlay,' he said, facing their captor and controlling his anger, 'I don't know what the devil you're about – but we can do with your help. We have the King of Spain. *Implacable*'s at Erdeven to take him off. If you're what you claimed to be last time we met –'

'We shall speak in French,' interrupted Verlay in that language. 'It is safer both for me and for you. And you are wrong, Monsieur Ring. *I* have the King of Spain.'

'Who is this man, Robert?' Jeanne demanded.

He answered without taking his eyes from Verlay. 'He's a secret agent of the British Government, engaged on a mission for the Foreign Secretary. Or so he's told me.'

'And with impeccable veracity,' Verlay agreed with a faint smile. 'As for what I'm about – but I beg your pardon, Mademoiselle Bonchamps, for my ill manners. I've looked forward to this meeting. I fear you are fatigued – captain, there are chairs by the wall and your man may place them for you.' His glance went to Turfrey, who was crouching with his fists clenched, watching Ring. 'You had better tell him to attempt no mischief. This is at half-cock –' he lifted a short-barrelled pistol from the table to display it – 'and I have men within call.'

Ring growled to Turfrey, 'Bring three chairs. We're flat aback on a lee shore, but by God I'll know the reason why!'

Verlay nodded at him, still with the faint smile on his thin lips. On the table before him, besides the pistol, were pen and inkwell, some sheets of paper on which he had been writing, a *carafe* of wine and a glass. His cocked hat was on the window-sill, his riding-cloak hung on the back of his chair. The fading light in the low-ceilinged, deep-windowed room showed a curious expression on his bony face, between complacency and wonder, as he surveyed the weary trio sitting before him. He poured wine into the glass, looking at Jeanne.

'Permit me, mademoiselle, to offer –'

'I don't drink wine with an enemy, monsieur,' she broke in with spirit. 'What have you done with the King? Where is he?'

'Ah.' Verlay lifted the glass and took a sip. 'There you trench upon the explanation I'm about to give you. Not that you deserve one. Your misguided efforts have given me more trouble than –'

He stopped speaking and cocked his head on one side, listening. From the yard outside came the rumble of wheels and the clatter of many hooves, fast receding.

'You ask where is the King of Spain, mademoiselle,' he resumed. 'He is in that carriage, with five mounted gendarmes for escort. He'll be at Vannes tonight, back at Valençay tomorow.'

'Why, you – you damned traitor!' Ring was on his feet. 'So you're Bonaparte's man after all! By God, I'd like to –'

'Sit down!' rasped Verlay, laying a hand on his pistol. 'And speak French, if you speak at all. You're here to listen to me, Monsieur Ring,' he went on as Ring sullenly resumed his seat, 'and when I've finished enlightening your ignorance you'll perceive that the word 'traitor' is meaningless in our present affair. Now – I've little time to spare. I've waited here for you since yesterday noon and my hours of grace are numbered. An emissary from Paris is expected in Nantes today, a man acquainted with the late genuine François Labiche, and my immediate need is to ride northward to the coast and leave the country. I shall therefore –'

'How did you know we would arrive here?' Jeanne interrupted. 'And where are Monsieur and Madame Kerzo?'

Verlay waggled a hand at her irritably. 'Pray allow me to talk, mademoiselle. Your friends the Kerzos are unharmed. As soon as I'm gone they will be allowed the freedom of their house again. As to my knowledge of your doings, you'll learn of that more quickly if you listen.'

He sat back in his chair and drank wine before continuing.

'*Bien*. The two boats left on the beach after the landing had meaning for me though not for the fool of an officer who ordered their destruction. The larger boat, identified by a fisherman of La Turballe as belonging to Mademoiselle Bonchamps of Houat, interested me so much that I crossed at once to Houat to learn what I could about it. My informant there was able to report a conversation he had overheard on board the Baron de Feriet's schooner.'

'Barac?' Jeanne cried. 'Alphonse Barac – a spy?'

Verlay shrugged. 'A paid agent, mademoiselle – I have many such. And let me assure you that Barac remains a devoted royalist. His pay comes from King George, not from the Emperor. But to resume. I now knew, firstly, that De Feriet's help had been enlisted for the rescue of the King of Spain – a possibility envisaged and already guarded against. Secondly, that the mill at Callac, a safe house, was to have been the probable goal for those who would embark at Erdeven. Thirdly, that some member or members of the Royal Navy, with or without the young woman from Houat, were at large on the French coast. I must confess that none of this seemed, at the time, of much importance. The Spaniards were taken. My business was done.' He looked at Ring. 'Of course, I didn't then know that you were involved.'

'Come to the point, man!' Ring growled. 'What concern had you with the Spaniards?'

'Patience, captain, patience,' Verlay drawled. 'I tell this tale in my own way. Well – four days ago the news of Ferdinand's escape reached Nantes. Two men and a woman had been seen with the King. I saw at once that the incredible had happened – and it was then, Monsieur Ring, that I suspected your hand in it. To me it seemed certain that Erdeven was the goal of these fugitives and that sooner or later they would – if they were not caught first – reach the mill at Callac. I rode for Callac at once with five gendarmes. You were watched for and the trap was set.' He spread his hands with a deprecatory smile. 'A little dramatic, you think? I have a taste for such things. And you'll agree it was a good deal neater than ambushing you on the forest path – where your big fellow there might have done some damage before he was held.'

He nodded towards Turfrey, who was sitting slumped in his chair with his eyes nearly closed, oblivious of talk that was wholly unintelligible to him. Ring felt fully as tired as Turfrey looked, but anger sustained him – anger that Verlay had not fully explained his actions. He was about to speak when Jeanne forestalled him. Her face, for the first time, showed lines of fatigue and anxiety; but she held herself upright and her brown eyes were wide and bright as she faced Verlay.

'Monsieur Verlay, if that is your name,' she said slowly and steadily, 'am I to understand that it was you who arranged the capture of the Baron de Kolli and Don Felicito Maura when they landed?'

'You are, mademoiselle. I did so by order from the Foreign Secretary in London, the Marquess –'

'That's a damned lie!' Ring snapped in English. '*Implacable*'s captain read to me the Marquess Wellesley's orders –'

He stopped as Jeanne laid a hand on his arm.

'One moment, Robert, if you please.' Her voice sounded oddly high and strained. 'Monsieur Verlay, did Yves de Feriet help you to entrap the Spaniards?'

Verlay frowned surprise. 'He, the smuggler-baron, the royalist? He would have hindered me, surely – but in any case he could do nothing. As I told you, I had guarded against the possibility. I hinted to the Préfect at Nantes that it might be a wise precaution to immobilise a gentleman known to have Chouan friends while we were catching Spanish royalists, and Monsieur de Feriet was respectfully but firmly required to stay within doors at the house in the Rue de la Boucherie. By now, no doubt, he is busying himself with his trade again – Mademoiselle,' he added quickly, 'you are ill. Some wine –'

'No.'

Jeanne spoke the word in a whisper. She was sitting rigid, tense, her eyes fixed in a blank stare. Verlay turned on Ring.

'From you, captain, I shall expect an apology. I have told no lie.'

'If you choose to resent it I'll meet you when and where you like.'

'*Imbécile!*' Verlay snarled exasperatedly; he lowered his voice and spoke rapidly in English. 'Ignorance is your trouble, Ring. You don't know that the Central Junta in Spain, which controls three out of the four Spanish armies, resolved last month that Spain should be a republic when they've kicked the French out. The monarchists were outvoted and so far they've taken it quietly – which is as well, since Wellington can't hold ground in the Peninsula without the help of those Spanish armies. But it's a powder-barrel and Ferdinand back in Spain could detonate it.'

'The Foreign Secretary agreed to aid Ferdinand's escape,' Ring muttered stubbornly.

'Of course!' Verlay cried. 'His Majesty's Government can't afford to alienate the monarchists. But what would happen if the exiled King of Spain suddenly reappeared in Madrid and raised the monarchist flag? Civil war, Ring – the end of Spanish help for Wellington – the French triumphant. So –' he shrugged – 'the mission to Valençay had to be aided, and it had to fail. The project was so flimsy that it was bound to fail, in my opinion.' He took a folded paper from the table, put it in his pocket, and stood up. 'My report states that my own mission, which was to ensure its failure, was successful.'

The sun was setting behind the forest that surrounded Callac and the room had darkened. A snore that was half a choke came from the dozing Turfrey. Jeanne, still sitting motionless, gave no sign that she heard when Verlay, cloak over arm and hat in hand, took his abrupt leave.

'Mademoiselle Bonchamps, adieu. Monsieur Ring, a word of advice. Stick to your schooner and don't meddle with matters on shore.'

He went out of the room by its inner door and his footsteps receded into the house. Voices, a man's and a woman's, rose in a clamour and Verlay's voice quelled it. A door slammed, a horse whinnied, hooves clattered and steadied into a canter that swiftly faded in the distance.

Ring got up stiffly and turned to Jeanne. Her shoulders were bowed and shaking and her head was sunk on her hands. He bent over her.

'Jeanne, *chérie* –'

The inner door burst open to admit a large man and a very stout woman, borne in on a wave of voluble exclamation that roused the slumbering Turfrey. Madame Kerzo, mob-cap awry on grey hair, caught Jeanne to her enormous bosom without pausing in her torrent of explanation and commiseration and bore her bodily from the room. Her bearded husband led Ring and Turfrey to a stone-flagged kitchen where firelight glinted on brass and copper and made them sit down at a scrubbed wooden table. Great bowls of soup were set before them and plates piled with maize-cakes and wheaten bread. Jeanne had disappeared; Madame Kerzo, with an accusing eye on Ring, declared that bed was the place for a girl in her state and she could take her soup there. Jean Kerzo exhausted an extensive vocabulary of oaths in condemnation of Bonaparte's officials in general and François Labiche in particular, pausing only to adjure his guests with '*mangez – mangez!*'

Ring saw and heard it all as in a dream. The accumulated toils and trials of the past nine days seemed to have descended upon his shoulders with crushing weight, and utter weariness, mental as well as physical, blunted all perception. Even the realisation of lost endeavour was hard to grasp. He was relieved when the miller waved aside his stumbling attempt to explain their journey, saying that it could wait till tomorrow. And the words that told Kerzo that they must start early tomorrow for the last stage of their journey to Erdeven seemed to be spoken by some voice other than his own.

When they had eaten the miller took them up to a loft smelling of hay, where there were two truckle-beds, and left them. Turfrey threw himself down and was snoring within half-a-minute. Ring, sitting on his bed, strove as he unbuttoned his coat to get his thoughts into some sort of order, but in vain. As his fingers fumbled with the last button he toppled over sideways and was asleep when his head touched the pillow.

When he woke, later than he had planned, the light of a bright morning was flooding through the high window of the loft. His mind was clear again and he could control his thoughts, pushing behind him useless repinings and concentrating as usual on the matter immediately in hand: the journey to Erdeven, food for the journey, advice from the miller as to the safest route. He gave Turfrey a shake and went down to the kitchen. Madame Kerzo was there stirring a pot of maize porridge on the fire. Ring gave her good morning and inquired whether Mademoiselle Bonchamps was yet up and about. She stared at him for a moment in silence, a curious expression on her wrinkled red face. Then she shrugged and pointed.

'You'd better look in the other room, monsieur. Mademoiselle was away before I'd left my bed. It's none of my affair but may the good Saint Gildas forgive me if I say the devil's in young girls nowadays when they go a-roaming without so much as a word of farewell or a by-your-leave –'

Ring left her talking and strode hastily to the room where they had sat with Verlay the evening before. Inkwell and pen were still on the table with some sheets of paper. One of the sheets bore a few lines of writing:

'I did him a terrible injustice. You will understand that I must go back to him. Please do not try to follow me.
Jeanne.'

3

Not a light showed on the dark waste of the Erdeven marsh that stretched away inland for two miles. The dark waste of the sea reaching to an invisible horizon in the opposite direction was equally lightless; but between the two, on the low dunes that separated marsh from shore, a red glow appeared fitfully between the black shoulders of sand. Turfrey's fire had been lit shortly before midnight on a ledge he had dug in the face of the dune nearest to the creeping tide, and on this seaward side it made so fine a blaze that the moving furrows of surf winked ruby-red in reflection.

Ring and Turfrey sat huddled in their cloaks beside the pile of driftwood Turfrey had collected. Neither had spoken since the fire had been lit half-an-hour ago, Ring because he was in no mood for talk and Turfrey because he had learned naval discipline. It was a silence that had been rarely broken during the day's journey that lay behind them.

The journey had been totally uneventful. The route given them by the miller – the forest trails, the winding paths of the heathland, the lonely lanes by which they had avoided the little town of Auray – had been followed without error or challenge; the few folk they met showed no interest in the two wayfarers and the harvesters in the fields near Auray did not even look up as they passed. Ring found no satisfaction in this. He missed the spur of danger, the challenge of difficulties, the excitement of evading pursuit. And he missed Jeanne. She was of the past now, he would never see her again, and it was not his way to dwell on matters that were over and done with; nevertheless, the road seemed doubly long and wearisome without her small gallant figure beside him. To rid his mind of memories he had occupied it with the future.

Every step brought him nearer to the sea, and there was great comfort in that. Ring had had his fill of the land, a dusty squalid place with its confined horizons and sluggish waters. To feel the lift and 'scend of a deck under his feet again, smell the salt breeze, see the blue rim of the world all round him – this was the proper stuff of living and he was going back to it. *Nonpareil* would have been sent home for repairs but she'd still be his – or would she? Would their Lordships at the Admiralty not break him when they heard of his barren adventurings 150 miles inside France? From one point of view he'd been guilty of dereliction of duty, for he had made no effort to rejoin his ship. His report to Cockburn needed careful consideration and he gave it that.

In the end he concluded that mere prudence required an abbreviated version of his ten-day absence, and if omission of a fact or two didn't count as lying it would be the truth. He and Turfrey, narrowly escaping capture when the Spaniards were taken, had been hunted from one place to another, hiding in barns and forests until they finally made their way to the point at Erdeven. He might add, perhaps, that they had been aided by a French girl.

But that addition in his thoughts brought him back to Jeanne again. For all that they had made love – in that most unromantic of bowers – his was not the sorrow of the heartbroken lover the poets sang about, Ring decided. He wouldn't forget the poignant sweetness of the moment when she gave herself to him; but what he missed was a companion, a comrade. That was her own word – comrade, and never, he told himself, did a man have a better one or a braver. No. His heart wasn't broken. But there was an empty space in it which he felt could never be filled. This melancholy mood had stayed with him as he followed Turfrey's skilful guidance across the black Erdeven marshes, and it was with him now as they sat by the signal-fire.

Turfrey placed another log of driftwood on the fire and sat down again in the sand. *Implacable* could come in to half-a-mile off shore here, but she would show no light and in any case the fire's glare made it useless to keep a lookout for her on a night as dark and clouded as this. The flaming driftwood crackled, the surf gently growled, and when Turfrey broke a long silence his voice scarcely rose above these sounds.

'This Sally Briggs an' me, we'd been sweethearts for nigh on a twelvemonth when she run off with a travellin' hoss-dealer.' He spoke as if he was talking to himself. 'Left me sick an' sorry, like. Ah, thinks I, 'tis the end. There'll be no other for me, long as I live. But 'tisn't so an' never was. Inside a fortnit I was swearin' black an' blue there wasn't a one in the world to compare with Liza.'

He made a long pause and Ring felt impelled to say something. 'You'd found another girl, I suppose.'

'Nay, sir – Liza was a lurcher bitch. Take a pheasant like a human, an' quieter, she could. Her an' me made a pair. When I was took an' hauled away to be a Navy seaman 'twas as bad as partin' from Sally. Worse, maybe. But it don't stay like that, sir. I've got another darlin' already, an' her name's *Nonbarrel*.' Turfrey hesitated. 'I've sometimes thought you felt same as me about her, sir,' he added diffidently.

Ring was silent for a moment. Then, with a sudden movement, he reached out his hand.

'You're a good fellow, Turfrey,' he said abruptly.

Turfrey gripped the hand briefly and turned away to feed the fire. In the act of breaking a stick he stopped and straightened himself to listen.

'Boat headin' inshore, sir,' he said.

Ring sprang to his feet and ran down to the water's edge. The onshore wind brought to his ears the steady creak and plash of oars.

'Boat ahoy!' he shouted.

'By God – that was Ring!' said a voice loudly; Ward's voice – and Ward's following yell. 'Whither bound, mister?'

'Homeward bound with a cargo of damn-all!' Ring shouted back.

And grinned wryly as he shouted. For once that was true.

Historical Note

Evidence of the Royal Navy's participation in a Spanish attempt to free Ferdinand VII from the Château de Valençay is to be found in *The Wellesley Papers*, pages 302 to 308, where the secret dispatches exchanged between Captain Cockburn of *Implacable* and the Marquess Wellesley are on record. The two agents, the Baron de Kolli and Don Felicito Maura, were duly landed on the French coast; nothing was ever heard of them again. Perhaps because the operation was a total failure, there is no mention of it in official naval histories.